"No one

SATURDAY'S
HEROES

LOW LIFE

To the Rainham End.

Saturday's Heroes (pbk)

© Joe Mitchell

ISBN 1 898928 05 3

Published by Low Life, Scotland.

Printed by Progressive, England.

This book is a work of fiction.
The characters and events are purely imaginary.
Any resemblance to real life is truly amazing.
There is no such place as Gillingham.

Low Life is an imprint of
S.T. Publishing, P.O. Box 12, Dunoon, Argyll. PA23 7BQ.
Scotland.

"No one likes us - we don't care"

SATURDAY'S
HEROES

A debut novel by Joe Mitchell

CHAPTER ONE

AS Paul West left the football ground, he knew there was little chance of any trouble. The fighting before the game guaranteed that the Old Bill would be out in force once the final whistle had blown, and that's exactly what happened. What made it worse though, was the fact that Paul and his crew had managed to attract the attention of two uniformed bobbies who followed the seven skinheads all the way to the train station.

It was amazing really. Skins hadn't ruled the terraces for a good four years, but you still couldn't go near a football ground with a crop and boots without the police fingering you as public enemy number one. Last season, at Walsall, Paul had been searched on four separate occasions going into the game, while a crew of about 50 casuals waltzed straight in without even a raised eyebrow from the plods on duty.

It looked like being one of those days. None of Paul's crew had even been involved in the trouble before the game. Tony had to work Saturday mornings in a timber merchant's yard, Simon stacked shelves down the Co-Op and the rest of them were down the pub as soon as it opened its doors. They hadn't left the Red Lion until five minutes before kick-off and had missed the first ten minutes of the match as well as the aggro in the town.

The two policemen followed them all the way down to the platform and watched the skinheads get into the very last carriage. Big Trev pulled down the window and started waving at them as if he was saying goodbye to a loved one.

"Get in here you dopey bastard!" Paul shouted. "It's bloody freezing with that window open!"

Big Trev slammed the window shut and took a seat opposite Paul.

"So, are we going for a quick pint when we get home or what?" asked Bill. He was a brewery on legs that one.

"Might as well. I'll have to wait until my Dad comes home at seven to get the van anyway", chipped in Alan.

Alan was a tall, thin bloke who was very handy to know. Not only could he use his father's Transit van to ferry everyone around, but he also seemed to know everyone who was anyone. If you wanted anything from a washer for a tap right up to a new video recorder, Alan was your man. No questions asked, no fancy shop prices to pay.

"Did you see that big fat bird standing behind the goal?" said Simon, trying to change the subject. He was only 15, looked even younger, and had no chance of getting served in a pub. His best hope was that the rest of them would give the pub a miss, get a few bottles from the off-licence and drink them over the park. "I missed the last two goals because of her fat arse!"

"You should have been watching the game instead of licking it then, you dirty little bastard!" came the quick reply from Bill. Everyone laughed, even Simon. He was the youngest member of the Medway Skinhead Syndicate and was the butt of more jokes than Les Dawson's mother-in-law. The rest of the mob were all in their early twenties and had all been skins since the late Seventies.

The train sat in the station for what seemed like ages. Then there was the sound of a lot of people running down the stairs, a dozen or more doors opened and slammed shut, and seconds later the shabby excuse for public transport was pulling away. Final destination London Charing Cross, but before that it had to pass through Chatham and Strood as well as a dozen or more other stops between the River Medway and the Big Smoke.

As soon as it had pulled clear of Gillingham station, the muffled choruses of football songs could be heard from the other end of the train. After a 3-1 win, it was the home fans who had most to sing about, but most of the Gillingham fans who got this train home after a game didn't even sing inside the ground. What's more, these songs seemed to be working their way slowly up towards the carriage the skinheads occupied along with a few old couples and a woman with a kid.

It soon became clear that the long delay at the station was to give Reading fans a chance to catch the train, and it was them who were making all the noise. They had been kept behind for a good ten minutes after the game, but once the gates had been opened it was in the interests of the police to get them off their patch and on to the first train available. Anything for a quiet life, the Old Bill, and who could blame them.

The chanting got nearer and nearer, until the door that separated the end carriage from the rest of the train opened. Then it was available to Paul and his mob in glorious stereo.

"Who wants to pay up and who wants slashed?" shouted the first voice to enter the carriage.

Paul could see the worried looks on the faces of the other passengers, but still couldn't see who was doing the mouthing. Obviously, the mouth hadn't seen the Gillingham fans either, but he soon heard them. Trev started them off with, "Gillingham! Gillingham! Gillingham!", and within three words the rest of the MSS had joined in and were banging the side of the train and stamping their boots on the dirty floor.

Darren hadn't collected so much as a penny before being momentarily stopped in his tracks by the battle cry now echoing around the carriage. He had already passed about 30 Gillingham fans as he made his way down the train with the other Reading casuals, but they'd all been scarfers, all too willing to hand over the contents of their pockets. Either there were a few simpletons in this last carriage who were about to suffer, or he had stumbled upon an excuse for a rival mob. Both possibilities put a smile on his face as he bypassed the pensioners and made his way down to where the noise was coming from.

By the time Darren saw the shaven heads of the opposition, he had been joined by another dozen or so casuals. Most were under-fives, young kids who still hadn't graduated to the full-time ranks of Reading's best dressed elite, but Jonesy and Big Ricky had seen active service at football grounds up and down the country.

It wasn't long before the chants of "Gillingham!" were being drowned out by "Nobody kicks the fuck out of you, like a Reading Casual Crew!", but it didn't shut the skinheads up. The casuals soon outnumbered the skins three to one, and the last thing the Gillingham lot wanted was a ruck in the confined space of the train. None of their lot were tooled up and they knew equally well that casuals loved to play the hard man with a blade. A war of words would keep the casuals at bay - at least for the time being.

The train would arrive at Chatham station within a minute or so. It wasn't their stop, but it was a certainty that the skinheads wouldn't survive until Strood without the slanging match turning into a full-scale battle. Paul nodded to his mates sitting opposite to let them know they were getting off earlier than usual, but he soon wished he hadn't. Simon was sitting nearest the door and when his hand moved towards the handle, with the train only just pulling into the station, it was seen as a sign of weakness by Darren and his fellow tax collectors.

"You're not leaving us already are you boys?" asked a spotty little git in a Pringle jumper.

"That's it. Run home to Mummy!" shouted another casual.

As the train came to a halt, the skinheads took their leave with the taunt of "Dinosaurs!" ringing in their ears. Simon couldn't get off quick enough, but the others did their best to leave at their own pace. Sensing victory, the Reading fans turned up the volume in the abuse stakes, but apart from the odd shove it looked like the Gillingham skins would live to fight another day.

Then, one of the younger casuals took a step forward and lashed out with a Stanley knife, catching Tony on his left cheek just as his first boot had touched down on the concrete platform. Instinctively Tony's hand went up and caught the first drops of blood.

9

"You bastard!" he shouted. He wanted to get back on the train and kick his attacker all the way back to Reading. He really wanted too, but he wouldn't have stood a chance. Spurred on by the sight of blood, the casuals were now hanging out of the carriage doors, giving it the big come on to the handful of Gillingham fans now crowding around Tony.

The strange thing was he didn't feel any pain, but the look on everyone's face told Tony that he had to see the damage for himself. He made his way to the toilet, with the chant of "Nobody kicks the fuck out of you, like a Reading Casual Crew!" drowning out the station announcer's message that the train wasn't leaving until all the doors were shut.

As Tony and the rest of the MSS entered the toilet they knew it just might be their day after all. One of the Reading casuals had left the train for a drink and was scooping water with his hands from a running tap. Before the boy could even look up, Tony had him by the hair and started to bang his scared-shitless face off the sink. The mixture of blood and running water soon turned the basin red, but still Tony didn't stop. Skin and bone were being smashed on to the cold stainless steel and Tony was loving every moment of it. This little bastard was going to pay for his slashed face and the blood stains on his fawn sheepskin.

For the casual it must have seemed like a lifetime, but Tony had done as much damage as he was likely to do in about thirty seconds flat. There was blood everywhere. How much damage had been done was anybody's guess. There was just too much blood to see if the luckless Reading fan even still had a face.

Still holding him by the hair, Tony dragged the screaming kid out of the toilet and threw him down on the platform, in full view of the train. And that was it. A red rag to a raging bull.

Doors the length of the platform flew open and the train began to empty. About a hundred Reading fans wanted to make amends for their fallen comrade. By then of course, Tony and the others were half way up the stairs and heading for the station exit. They shot past the startled ticket collector, with only Paul momentarily stopping to tell the fat bastard to shut the gates.

Nobody had time to wait and see if he would close them or not, but after five minutes of running it was obvious that they had made good their escape. By then they had reached the shopping centre and there was no way any Reading fans would risk going that far from their ride home. Not if they had a brain between them anyway.

Despite being ran, the MSS were claiming victory. Against all the odds, they'd managed to teach at least one of Reading's dressers a lesson he'd not forget in a hurry. No doubt the train to London was full of similar talk of how Gillingham had been fleeced on their own turf. The eighty odd quid they'd collected by steaming the train would certainly pay for a big celebration back home anyway.

Now inside the Rose & Crown, Tony joined in the verbal action replays, but only after 'phoning for a taxi to take him to the hospital. He knew he'd need stitches, but at least it was a clean cut. The latest craze was to use two blades taped close to each other so that it was really difficult for doctors to repair the damage.

11

Luckily for Tony, that was still to catch on amongst sheep shaggers like Reading.

"Did you see the ticket collector's face when we ran by?", Trev asked with a smile on his face. "Poor bastard nearly had a heart attack!"

"So did I when I saw that fucking train empty!" shouted Bill, who had taken up his usual residence over by the fruit machine. He fed pound after pound into its obliging slot night after night, and then had to tap off the others for drinks when he came back empty handed. He was always trying to come up with a system that would guarantee wins, but from what the others could tell he hadn't even sussed out how the nudges worked. Stupid git.

So, we still on for tonight?" asked Alan.

"You can count me out. My face is fucking killing me," replied Tony.

The others were all up for it though. It wasn't every weekend that a decent dance was held within spitting distance and nobody could think of a better way to round off the day.

CHAPTER TWO

IT was raining. It was always raining these days, but tonight it was really coming down. Cats and dogs didn't get a look in. This was more like elephants and hippos. Paul stood just inside the entrance to the block of flats and waited for the van to arrive. He'd been standing there for twenty minutes, but should have known that bastard Alan would be late.

Eventually the Ford Transit came around the corner and came to a halt outside the flats. Paul turned up the collar to his crombie and started a mad dash towards the van and its empty passenger seat. Crombies might be smart and warm, but if they get wet they stink to high heaven, and Paul knew no bird would look twice at him if he smelt worse than a greaser. Except a greaser's bird of course.

When he reached the door, Paul tried to open it, then tried it again when it failed to open. Suddenly, the whole van erupted in laughter. Obviously seeing Alan getting a soaking was some wanker's idea of a joke. Eventually a hand lent over from the back of the van, unlocked the door, and Paul was able to claim his seat in the front next to Alan.

"Still raining is it Paul?" asked Simon from his place in the back of the van. A new burst of laughter provided the answer.

There were 12 people squeezed into the old white Transit. It had no seats in the back so nearly everyone had to make do with the cold metal floor. Apart from Simon and Colin who had a wheel arch each, only Pete did his best to crouch down instead of sprawl out -

because he "didn't want to get my suit dirty". Bloody poof.

Paul was glad not to be rattling around in the back with the others. He wasn't scared of a bit of dirt, but all the same, he did like his comfort. Plus it meant he had total control of the tape deck which was soon belting out some classic Motown tunes. Another twenty minutes and they'd be there.

* * *

Carol hated arriving early at dances. It was like being the first to arrive at a party - sod all to do except wait for others to turn up. Still, at least they had the pick of the tables to sit at and Debbie seemed happy enough.

Carol and Debbie were skingirls. Both were dressed in Levi's, brogues and plain shirts, one a Brutus and the other a Permanent Press Slimfit. They had first met three years ago while on holiday in Majorca with their families, had got on like a house on fire, and had kept in touch ever since. Carol was actually from Hull, but came to visit Debbie two or three times a year. Usually, she only came for the weekend, but this time they had both arranged for a week off work and were making a holiday of it.

Debbie had just lit her second fag of the night, when Paul and the other Medway skinheads walked through the door. By then, the room behind the pub was filling up nicely and it looked like the dance would be a success. The Joyriders Scooter Club had organised it, and by the looks of things they had attracted every skinhead, mod and scooterist within

14

travelling distance. Not to mention the two middle aged couples who'd paid to get in and left three minutes later when they realised this wasn't quite the Saturday night out they had in mind.

"Where's Tony?" asked Debbie as Paul approached the table.

"He ain't coming. He got into a bit of trouble after the football and decided to stay at home." Paul could see the worried look on Debbie's face so he added, "It's nothing serious and he said you'd to give him a call when I saw you."

Debbie had been going out with Tony since school. She was two years younger than him and they'd got engaged a few weeks ago on her nineteenth birthday.

"This is Carol," said Debbie, introducing her to the gang of skinheads who had descended on their table. "She's my friend from Hull so someone can buy us both a drink while I go and 'phone that idiot, Tony. Mine's a half cider."

As soon as Debbie left the table and Barry had been despatched to the bar, Paul introduced himself to Carol. "So what brings you down here then?" he asked, giving it the usual small talk.

"I'm staying with Debbie for a week. Better than spending my week off work at home!"

"So when do you go back then?"

"Give me a chance," Carol said, smiling. "I only got here yesterday and you're trying to get rid off me!"

Paul laughed. "No, nothing like that. There ain't enough skinhead girls around here at the best of times."

There was something about Carol that was almost magnetic. Her deep blue eyes had a lot to do

15

with it. Whenever Paul looked at her, they held his glance for just a moment longer than they should have done. Almost bordering on the uncomfortable, but at the same time pulling in Paul like a fish on a line. And Paul, naturally enough, was loving it.

They seemed to hit it off straight away. This girl certainly wasn't just a pretty face, and to think he nearly gave tonight a body swerve to stay in and watch the boxing on TV.

Derrick Morgan's *Fat Man* hit the turntable and within seconds the dancefloor was full of skinheads. Paul asked Carol if she fancied a twirl and they were soon dancing away with the rest of them. After a minute or so, they were joined by Debbie who was cursing Tony upside down.

For the next half hour or so, skinhead reggae ruled the DJ booth and the threesome never left the floor. Debbie kept saying things into Carol's ear while they both smiled in Tony's direction - making the poor sod feel more self-conscious than the owner of a two inch dick in a communal shower. Debbie was obviously letting her friend know what she was in for if she wanted to get involved with the skinhead stomping away before their eyes.

A psychobilly tune signalled the chance for a breather and as they walked back to the table, Carol grabbed Paul's arm and said, "Debbie and Tony are taking me out for a drink tomorrow night. Do you fancy coming along?"

"Yeah, that would be great," said Paul, relieved that he wouldn't have to try any of his two-bit chat up lines to get to see her again. "I'll make sure they take you to a decent boozer too, and not that trendy hole they'll have you drinking in."

More drinks were soon called for, so Paul headed for the bar. On his way he passed Big Trev, who wasn't doing too badly himself with a mod bird called Tracy. Trev had his arm around her shoulders and Paul just couldn't resist it. Coming up behind them, he lifted Trev's arm with his left hand and at the same time groped the girl's arse with his right, leaving the poor girl to think that Trev was coming on a bit strong all of a sudden. Not that she seemed to complain mind you.

Up at the bar, it took Paul ages to get served. By the time the barman started ringing up his order on one of those fancy tills that tells you what drinks you've ordered, Madness' version of the old Prince Buster classic, *One Step Beyond*, was blasting out of the speakers. He turned around just in time to see Debbie and Carol hit the dancefloor, but his attention was quickly drawn away from the girls and towards the far end of the room.

About a dozen skinheads had just arrived, but they were no friends of his. This lot were nothing more than bald punks in Paul's eyes, and their brand of Nazi politics did nothing for him. Of course, the baldies had Paul and his mates down as commies, but that wasn't the case at all. Every one of the Medway Skinhead Syndicate considered themselves patriotic and wouldn't have a word said against England. And to the MSS, sieg heiling and worshipping Adolf Hitler had sweet F.A. to do with being British and proud of it. Two World Wars and one World Cup, and you still had idiots backing the losing side.

The scooterist standing next to Paul at the bar tapped him on the shoulder. "If it goes off, our lot will back you up no problem."

"Cheers mate," Paul replied, but he was more concerned by what was happening on the dancefloor. It was clearing as quickly as it did that night someone put on a Duran Duran record as a joke, but this time nobody was laughing. Three of the MSS, Alan, Bill and Wayne, had gone over to the boneheads and it was obvious to all that words were being had.

Paul caught Simon's eye and called him over. The young skinhead was told to take the drinks to the table and Paul walked across the now empty dancefloor to see what the score was.

"We ain't after any trouble. We've just come for a night out," said one of the boneheads.

"Yeah, well you make the place look untidy," said Alan. "And we don't want your sort here."

By now the Joyriders' number one had come over to see if he could calm things down, but this dance wasn't big enough for both skinhead mobs. Not as far as the Syndicate boys were concerned anyway.

"We paid to get in, nobody else wants us to leave and we're staying," said the same bonehead, who was obviously something of a leader of this little lot.

"Either you walk back down those stairs or I'll personally throw you down them," said Wayne.

"You think you're so fucking hard don't you?" said another baldy in black pilot jacket, combat trousers and knee high boots. By then the music had stopped and the noise of Wayne's forehead cracking into his face was the only sound to break the silence.

Within seconds, the other MSS skins were steaming towards the boneheads, chanting "Syndicate! Syndicate! Syndicate!" and showering them in chairs, glasses and bottles.

Number-wise the mobs were fairly even, but the Nazis didn't stand a chance. A few of them were handy enough and wanted to know, but they weren't a unit and it was every man for himself. In the opposite corner were the MSS, a football mob. They had stood and fought together since school, and had the master race on the retreat from the word go.

One bonehead who had been decked by a flying chair was being kicked senseless by two of the MSS, and his mates weren't fairing much better. Three of them just didn't want to know and had made for the stairs, leaving their mates to take their share of the kicking. Paul had run into one, fists flying, and he didn't take a single hit in reply. Colin was the only one who looked like he'd met his match when a nasty piece of work started getting the better of him, but Big Trev soon tipped the balance the other way by smashing a glass into the bonehead's face.

It was all over in a matter of minutes, as most rucks usually are. The bouncers had waited in the wings until it had quietened down before making a late entry in the peace stakes, but with their appearance the MSS moved away, taking up a position in the middle of the dancefloor. Not that the rival mob wanted to know any more. That boy on the floor wasn't even moving and was a certain candidate for an ambulance.

The aggro had obviously sickened a lot of those present. Most had come out for a drink and a laugh, and nothing else. Several girls were crying, and to their amazement the MSS found themselves being shunned by those who stood around the edges of the dancefloor. People were blaming them for ruining what should have been a trouble-free night out. And one of those jeering the loudest was the very same scooterist who had offered his club's support up at the bar.

Paul couldn't believe the reaction the MSS were getting. He just couldn't fucking believe it. He was certainly in no mood to apologise. When the voice through the speakers asked him and his mates to leave, and a cheer went up, that was about as much as he was going to take. The MSS chant went up again, and Paul started giving the two-faced scooterist hand signals to join him on the dancefloor. "Come on then, come on!" Paul shouted.

He started moving towards the scooterist, but before he could reach him, Simon flew by and whacked the bastard in the face. Even little Simon was doing the fucking business! The crowd backed away, knocking a table and its drinks over as they did so. A few of those at the front got a slap for their troubles, but nobody wanted to know - not even the bouncers - and the power felt by a dozen members of the famous Medway Skinhead Syndicate was electrifying. For the next few minutes they ruled that club, and only an announcement that the police had been called ended their reign.

With the old Millwall chant of "No one likes us!" to the tune of Rod Stewart's *Sailing*, the MSS bid farewell and headed down the stairs into the cold night air, but still the night's aggro wasn't over. As they stepped out of the club's doorway, they were greeted by a hail of bottles and stones. It might have been more threatening if every single missile hadn't fallen a hundred yards short, but the mugs throwing them were standing far too far away to hit their targets.

A cry went up, and the MSS were soon running up towards the boneheads at the top of the street. A few more bottles came flying, but the enemy was soon on its toes and heading off down a side street. And who could blame them? On another night, they might be lucky and turn the tables, but this time around they were backing a loser all the way.

Four of five trendies came out of a chip shop to see what was happening, and when the MSS gave up the chase they turned their attention to this little firm. They had no intention of running them, but a song at the very least was called for - just so they knew exactly who the victors were in the battle of the skinheads.

"Stand! Stand! If you think you're the best,
We are the famous MSS,
And we don't give a fuck whoever you may be,
For we are the famous GFC!"

Believing discretion to be the better part of valour, the casuals disappeared back inside the chippy, leaving the skinhead choir to continue on its way. And that's when Paul saw Debbie and Carol getting into a taxi.

Fuck, he'd forgotten all about them when the fight started. He shouted after them, but they either didn't hear him or didn't want to, because the door slammed shut and the taxi was off on its way.

"Don't worry, Westy boy. There's plenty more fish in the sea," said Alan, putting his arm around his mate's shoulder.

Paul laughed and acted as if he couldn't care less, but he knew fine well that he wasn't interested in anybody else. Not now he'd met the girl of his dreams. He just hoped that drink tomorrow night was still on the cards.

When the taxi pulled up at Debbie's house, the two girls scraped together the two quid fare and bid the driver goodnight. As they walked down the path, Debbie put her arm around Carol to guide her indoors. There were no lights on so her Mum and Dad must have gone to bed early.

Once inside, Debbie made them a cup of tea each and they sat down at the kitchen table to drink it.

"If I'd have known there was going to be trouble I wouldn't have gone," said Debbie, happier now that they were away from the club.

"It wasn't your fault. I was having a great time until all the fighting started."

"Just wait until I see Tony", Debbie said, pausing to suck on her cigarette. "Mind you, if he'd been there it would have been no different. He would have waded in with the others and then disappeared, leaving me to face the music. Did you hear what that scooter girl called me?"

Carol laughed. Debbie was like an old mother hen, and her nineteen going on forty routine always put a smile on her face. "Do you think Paul will still come tomorrow?"

"Not if he knows what's good for him he won't," replied Debbie, "But that's never stopped him before. Anyway, I thought you were meant to be getting married in a few months?"

22

"Nothing wrong with having a final fling then is there?" Carol said as she picked up her mug of tea and took a long sip.

* * *

Paul lay on his bed, staring into space. It wasn't much of a room. An old single bed, a wardrobe and a chest of drawers, were the only sticks of furniture. One of the walls was covered in newspaper cuttings of bank holiday battles, football violence and other skinhead horror stories. Another had a poster of the Gillingham team on it, with a blue satin scarf pinned above it with the club's name on it - just in case somebody thought it was Everton or Chelsea.

Not that anybody was likely to be in his room. The only people who came to his block of flats were the people who lived there, and Paul didn't want any of them visiting him. The only ones he had any time for were the old folk. In fact he felt sorry for the poor bastards who were condemned to spend the last years of their lives in this concrete hell-hole.

The lift hadn't worked for as long as he could remember, and stairways and landings were covered in graffiti, litter and dog shit. Worst of all though were the needles that the junkies left behind. To Paul, the druggies were scum, low life who deserved a slow and painful death. To him they were no better than the pushers, rapists and other assorted perverts who polluted today's society.

The story went that the council didn't want to spend any money on the flats because they wanted to knock them down and build decent housing. Only they couldn't afford to bring in the demolition boys either. So the flats were left to those who couldn't get away and to the problem cases the council dumped there. It was hard enough being at the bottom of the housing ladder, but when they pull the ladder away, you just don't have a chance. Welcome to Alcatraz!

All of a sudden, Paul could hear voices from beyond the flat's front door. He sat up quickly and reached out for his baseball bat. Most nights it was the same. Druggies going up and down the stairs, trying doors in the hope of finding one unlocked. You could hear the bastards turning your handle and pushing against the lock. It scared the shit out of Paul so God knows what it did to the old people living on their own.

Less than a year ago, an old woman of 87 had been raped and beaten by an attacker or attackers who had broken into her flat in the afternoon. In broad daylight for fuck's sake. She had been found dead two weeks later by a social worker on a routine visit. Only the lowest of the low steal from their own kind, but it took the ultimate in scum to do something like that.

Tonight, the druggies had given Paul's door a miss and he could hear them going down the stairwell, their voices fading as they went. It soon went quiet again, but Paul still couldn't sleep. His mind was working overtime and all he could think about was Carol.

They had been getting on so well. If only those fucking Nazis hadn't turned up it would have been a different story. Thoughts like that were doing his head in, so he tried to focus on something else by flicking through the latest copy of *Hard As Nails* which had arrived yesterday morning. Usually this little fanzine

24

kept him busy for ages, but he just wasn't in the mood. Even the Foxy Chick page received only a few seconds of his time.

He put it back under his bed, switched off the light and closed his eyes. He ended up tossing and turning for the next few minutes, but the sandman caught up with him sooner rather than later, and within a quarter of an hour the only noise breaking the night's silence was his snoring.

CHAPTER THREE

BY the time Paul walked into the pub, Tony, Debbie and Carol had already had a drink and Tony was up at the bar buying another round. "Just in time, mate. A pint of best?"

"Yeah, cheers mate," replied Paul. "How's your face?"

"Sore!" laughed Tony, as he turned to show Paul the neat line of stitches running down his left cheek. "I had this stupid patch thing on it until this morning, but there was no way I was going out on the drink with that covering half me face."

Tony paid for the drinks and the two skinheads walked over to where the girls were sitting. Paul was half expecting a roasting or at least a mention of the trouble on Saturday, but after the usual greetings the conversation turned to the more important subject of crisps and people's favourite flavours.

It was as if the dance had gone off without incident. An hour or so later, when Debbie and Carol disappeared to the toilets together, Paul asked Tony if Debbie had told him about the aggro on Saturday night.

"Told me? You'd have thought I'd started it the way she's been going on! Carol wasn't very impressed either from what Debs was saying."

"What was the big problem? Debbie knows the score. What were we meant to do - buy them bastards drinks all night?"

Tony saw the girls coming back. "Fuck knows, mate. Did you hear Simon has got himself a 50 Special?"

The girls were back at the table and Paul took it that Tony's sudden change of conversation meant that it was best to shut up about the fight while they were there.

For the next couple of hours, the four skinheads sat at the table, talking about this and that. Carol was a really good laugh, and Paul found himself falling head over heels in love with her. She was everything he ever wanted in a girl. Perfectly turned out in shirt, mini-skirt, fishnets and loafers, a really soft feather-cut, a great figure and those piercing blue eyes. So deep and blue you could almost swim in them.

What with talk about Hull being by the coast and then bank holiday beanos to the seaside, Debbie had a thought. "Why don't we all go to Folkestone tomorrow?"

"Tomorrow? " asked Tony, a bit surprised. "It's all right for you lot, but some of us have to work for a living!"

"Take the day off. Phone in sick," suggested Debbie. "I'll ring up and say you've got the 'flu."

"What do you reckon?" Tony asked Paul.

Paul was between jobs as they say, and the idea of a full day spent in the company of Carol was right up his street. "Yeah, I'm up for it. Should be a laugh."

"Okay, then. I'll pick Debbie and Carol up and meet you outside your flats about half nine. Howzat?"

"Sounds good to me. To Folkestone it is!" said Paul, lifting his glass so that the others could toast their day out. All four glasses met over the table.

"Right, we'd better finish these and get off home for our beauty sleep," Debbie said.

"Speak for yourself!" replied Tony, a comment that earned him a kick in the shin from his better half.

As they left the pub, Tony put his arm around Debbie and started walking off in front. It was a lot colder now and Carol shivered as she zipped up her Harrington.

"Do you want my jacket?" asked Paul, who still believed that girls liked a bit of chivalry. Holding doors open, flowers, and all that.

"No, it's okay," said Carol who chose to put her arm around Paul's waist instead and snuggle up to him for warmth. Paul put his arm around her shoulder, holding her tightly as they walked off behind the other couple.

"Have you been to Folkestone before?" Carol asked.

"Yeah, loads of times. I used to go there quite a bit in the summer holidays when I was still at school. It's not quite Majorca, but at least they speak English!" Paul was picking up on the stories Debbie and Carol were telling earlier on about how they had first met.

"I'd love to be there now," said Carol dreamily. "All that sun!"

"Would you take me with you?" Paul asked, stopping and turning to look at her face to face.

"Yeah, I would", came the coy reply. Their eyes met and as he held her gaze, Paul leant forward and kissed her. They kissed, lips to lips, and then again, this time with Paul's tongue inside Carol's mouth. His hands slid down her sides, brushing past her tits and down to her waist. Her's remained around his neck.

"Come on you two!" shouted Tony, and for the first time the lovebirds realised they had an audience.

They kissed again, then hand in hand, they started to catch up with Debbie and Tony.

"You do know he's married with two kids, don't you?" Tony said to Carol, winking as he did so.

They all laughed and continued on their way towards Debbie's house.

The trip down to Folkestone was uneventful. The two boys sat in the front, the two girls in the back, and The Business' *Suburban Rebels* album provided the backing music courtesy of a tape in the car stereo. It might have been an old Vauxhall Viva that had seen better days, but Tony certainly hadn't settled for anything less than the best in in-car entertainment systems. In fact it was the best Mercedes had to offer. Or at least, the best the Mercedes that he'd nicked it from had to offer anyway.

They parked up in the big pay and display car park underneath Leas Cliff, and then crossed the road to the amusements. It was a bitter cold day, and since they had come out of season, not all the rides were operating. Still, it didn't stop them having a go at the crazy golf - which saw the girls claim victory despite the often dubious efforts of the blokes to win. Then they retired to the relative warmth of the arcade that shielded them from the cold winds coming in off the English Channel.

"Are you going to play at Nigel Mansell all day?" Debbie asked Tony as he put more money into the sit-in racing car game.

Paul and Carol were a few machines away, playing an arcade game called Track And Field which recreated all the excitement of the Olympic games. Well, that was the idea anyway. Paul had just recorded an 80m javelin throw when he heard Debbie complain.

"Shall we go and get something to eat?" he called over. "All this exercise has given me an appetite."

"I hope it hasn't sapped all your strength", said Carol, hinting heavily that he might need some for later on.

"Why? What did you have in mind?" asked Paul, looking for further conformation that his luck would be in today.

"Invite me home with you tonight and you'll find out won't you", she replied, and with that she turned and walked over to Debbie.

"Fuck this!", shouted Tony as his car went skidding off the track and into the crash barrier. "This steering wheel's faulty. I had that corner judged perfectly."

With the GAME OVER legend flashing away, Tony took his Doc Marten boot off the acceleration pedal and returned to the land of reality. All four of them then bid farewell to the arcade and headed along the seafront towards the town centre.

They stopped at a chippy for something to eat and then headed for the warm welcoming glow of the nearest pub. It was full of old suits with their young secretaries, no doubt enjoying a bar meal and a few drinks on their respective expense accounts. There wasn't a spare table to be had, so the skinheads made do with bar stools while they planned what they were going to do in the afternoon.

"There's no way I'm walking about out there," complained Debbie. "It's freezing. Does anybody fancy going to the cinema?"

"Why, what's on?" asked Paul.

"How the fuck should I know, but we could take a look," Debbie told him, making it clear that as far as she was concerned the cinema it was.

"Okay then," said Carol.

The two blokes just looked at each other. If the girls wanted to go to the cinema, then the cinema it was.

The choice of films wasn't exactly earth-shattering, and Paul found himself watching *Ghostbusters* with a grand total of seven other people. And that included Tony and Debbie who were sitting a few seats away from him and Carol on the same row. Not that he was really concentrating on the film.

Paul was sitting with his flight jacket on his lap, and within minutes of the film starting Carol's hand had found its way under it, and was stroking his groin through his jeans. His hands were wandering too, stroking her breasts underneath her Fred Perry jumper. Maybe *Ghostbusters* was well worth seeing after all.

Soon his jeans had been unbuttoned, his fly pulled down and Carol was massaging his dick between her fingers. "I hope you've got something for this to wear tonight," Carol whispered.

Paul replied by squeezing her other hand, before delving beneath her ski-pants. He was soon stroking her pubic hair, and then reaching further inside her knickers, to touch her fanny. For the best part of the film, they sat there, caressing and stroking each other.

All Paul could think about was coming. He was so close to exploding that he felt a nose bleed coming on.

With the film over, Paul hurriedly did his jeans back up. The lights came on, and as he stood up, he did his best to hide his bulging manhood by putting his hand in his pocket and carrying his flight jacket at waist height.

It took a full five minutes for his hard-on to disappear, leaving him to pretend he couldn't feel the cold as he walked back to the car - jacket still in hand.

Carol meanwhile was walking with Debbie, leaving him and Tony to bring up the rear.

"Enjoy that did you?" Tony asked.

"What?" said Paul, thinking that Tony and Debbie must have seen him and Carol fondling each other like dogs on heat.

"Hello, is there anybody in there? Did you enjoy the film you pillock?"

Paul laughed. "Best film I've been to in ages."

It was just after eleven when Paul opened the door to the flat. They had spent the evening in the pub listening to Billy boy talking about his latest plan to beat the fruit machines. Paul had missed part of it playing pool with Carol, but it had something to do with overheating the credit mechanism in the back of the machine by holding a lighter to it, and then playing free all night until the jackpot came up. "I'll be making two hundred easy, every week for just a couple of night's work", he boasted at one point. His only problem was finding a pub where he could hang about the machine with a lighter in his hand without getting the landlord's size ten up his arse.

Only the hall light was on, which meant Paul's Mum had gone to bed. She had lived on a diet of tranquillisers and sleeping pills for the last ten years, ever since his Dad died of a heart attack, so she would be out for the count for sure. Just as well really, because the noise coming from the flat upstairs would have disturbed anyone else's sleep.

"Those bastards are always playing that shit music until two or three in the morning," explained Paul, finding himself apologising on behalf of the scum who lived above him.

Paul might not have been working at the time, but the four blokes who shared the flat above hadn't done a day's work between them in their lives. And were never likely to either. Nobody wanted to employ grebo punks like them.

The strangest thing of all though wasn't that these bastards had nothing better to do except blare out crap in the early hours, but that nobody had ever done anything about it. And more to the point, Paul had done nothing about it. He had lost count of the times he had been kept awake by the constant pounding of music, but had never once gone up and sorted it. True, he'd banged on the ceiling with his baseball bat, but that did fuck all to stop the noise.

"Don't worry about it," said Carol, trying to lessen his obvious embarrassment. "You should hear the racket my little sister makes with her Wham! tapes."

He didn't say anything, but it wasn't the same. These bastards were invading his flat at whatever time they liked with their noise, and making his life a misery.

The constant fear that he would be woken up by it any night of the week was almost as bad as the drug takers prowling the landings after dark. It wasn't so much the music - he couldn't even hear what music it was - just the constant pounding. Just like when someone sits opposite you on a train with their Walkman on, and you can hear enough to know it's on, but not enough to know what's being played. Just like that, but louder. And yet, he was letting them get away with it. So much for an Englishman's home being his castle.

When they reached Paul's room, he switched on the old record player he had had for years, and put on a *Motown Chartbusters* LP. He had it turned down low, but it was still enough to drown out most of what was coming from upstairs.

Carol was sitting on his bed by the time he had neatly put the record sleeve away. As he went over to her, she stood up and they began to kiss and cuddle. The kissing became more passionate as his hands began to explore her body, starting with her breasts and working down towards her ski-pants. Carol had unbuttoned his Ben Sherman and was soon running her hands over his bare chest and stomach. Her touch was so gentle, so sensuous.

It wasn't long before they were undressing each other, and Carol was once again stroking his manhood. Only this time, she started kissing his neck and working her way down his body until she was kissing his now throbbing dick. All the touching and caressing in the cinema came flooding back, and all Paul wanted to do was come.

He started moving his dick in and out of her mouth, feeling her lips and tongue working away. He started moving faster and faster, and Carol's kissing and licking became more and more passionate. Barely two songs into the album and Paul was holding on to Carol's head as his dick started to shoot spunk inside her mouth. The moment of relief and ultimate pleasure couldn't come soon enough now. He had had blow-jobs before, but this was the best bar none . . .

Now it was Paul's turn to keep Carol satisfied while his dick recovered. He sat her down on the edge of the bed and started kissing her. First on the lips and then on her small, firm tits. Her nipples stood out as he kissed and sucked them. Her skin was as smooth as silk. She was groaning with pleasure by the time his hands made their way up her inner-thighs and started caressing her wet vagina. They were soon joined by his tongue which started probing away while his fingers went right inside her.

Carol lay back on the bed, her legs wide apart and hanging off the edge, and her arms spread out in total abandonment. She was moving her hips in rhythm to Paul's fingers going in and out of her fanny. Her moans and groans were really turning him on and within minutes his cock was hard again.

Still fingering her, he reached over to the battered chest of drawers, pulled open the top one and reached inside for a pack of Featherlite. Carol sat up, insisted that he continued to pet her and then pulled the only Durex in the box over Paul's prick. Within seconds he was on top of her and inside her. They were kissing passionately, her fingernails running riot over his back as they made love on the squeaking single bed.

It was now three in the morning and the only sound breaking the silence of the night was Paul and Carol whispering to one another. They had lay there for the last few hours talking about their lives, their thoughts and their dreams. And the more they talked, the more certain Paul was that this was the girl for him.

"Do you really have to go back on Thursday?" asked Paul.

"Yeah, I'm afraid so," replied Carol. "It's my Mum and Dad's wedding anniversary on the Saturday and then it's back to work on Monday."

"I can't believe I've met someone like you and am going to lose you after only a few days."

"Well, you can always come back to Hull with me, " said Carol her fingers stroking his chest, and then she laughed. "I could put you in my suitcase and smuggle you on to the coach!"

The way Paul was feeling it didn't sound such a bad idea. Not so much the suitcase bit, but going to Hull. After all he had no job to keep in him in the Medway towns and he could always come back to visit his Mum. And if it meant he would be able to see Carol, he would go to Timbuktu and back.

"Maybe I'll save up some money and move up to Hull," he said.

"That would be great," said Carol, kissing him on his chest where her head was now resting.

"What's it like for work?" Paul asked as he began to warm to the idea of moving north.

"You could easily get work on the ferries. They are always looking for people."

Paul didn't consider himself much of a seafarer - the school certificate for doing ten lengths at the swimming baths was about his limit - but a job was a job in Thatcher's Britain. And the ferries could just be the start of a decent career for a bloke who had done a hundred and one unconnected jobs since leaving school.

"When you get back, let me know what the score is and meantime I'll get some casual work and get some money together."

"Okay, sailor boy," replied Carol. Then turning towards him and climbing on top of him, she added, "Now, make love to me again . . . "

She started kissing him and fondling him, quickly bringing his dick to attention. Then she started rubbing it along her moist vagina.

"What about a johnny?" asked Paul, but he didn't have to wait for an answer. Carol had already inserted his dick deep inside her and once again they were performing the old in out . . .

CHAPTER FOUR

"HULL? What the fuck are you talking about? Hull?!"

Tuesday evening was always put aside for the Syndicate to talk about what was happening on the coming Saturday. A trip to Bolton was top of the agenda, but while they were waiting for Tony to arrive, Paul had made the mistake of mentioning that he might be going to Hull. Bobby was obviously not impressed. Neither was Alan.

"You've only known the bird five minutes and you want to move in with her? You've fucking flipped, Westy. They're all northern bastards up there!"

"Look, forget I mentioned it," replied Paul angrily. "All I said was I might be going to Hull for some work. That's all. Now can we talk about something else?"

"A whippet. You'll need to buy a whippet or you'll stick out like a sore thumb," laughed Bobby, wanting to get another dig in before the subject was dropped.

Ignoring him, Paul said, "So how many of us are going on Saturday then?"

Bobby reeled off a mental list. "Me, you, Alan, Tony if he's up to it, Trevor and Billy. Wayne says he doesn't have the money."

"What about the others?" demanded Trev.

"The usual excuses. Bloody part-timers," explained Alan. "Simon's Dad won't let him out of the house because he got in too late on Saturday. He gave the poor kid a clip around the ear too by the sound of things."

"We're going to scare the shit out of Bolton then, all six of us," added Big Trev. "Fucking wasters half this mob. Anyone can defend their own end. What we need is a decent away squad."

"Oh, well," said Billy as he stood up. "Hopefully some of the casuals will help us do the business." And on that optimistic note he went to the bar to get some change for the fruit machine.

As per usual though, Billy was talking out of a hole in his arse. Gillingham didn't have a casual mob. Not unless you counted the twenty or so ski-hats who stood at the Rainham End at home games, but they were under-five material and hadn't been seen at an away game all season.

Away from home, the Gills couldn't count on the sizeable gypsy support that turned up for home games either. Now they would make an away squad to be proud of. No, if it kicked off at Bolton, the only ones defending the good name of the Medway Towns would be the MSS and the thirty or so other hooligans who you could guarantee would turn up. Hardly enough to attract attention, let alone turn over Bolton's main firm on their own patch.

Just as Billy sunk his first ten pence piece into the machine's black hole, in walked Tony, Debbie and Carol. They pulled up some chairs and joined the other skinheads at the table over by the juke box.

Paul had last seen Carol when he said goodbye to her that morning before she left his flat to go back to Debbie's. And she looked more stunning than ever tonight in her tonic suit, shirt and fishnets. The way some of the other blokes were looking at her, he wasn't the only one who thought that either. The worse thing about being a skinhead in the mid-Eighties had to be the lack of decent looking skinhead birds to knock around with.

"Get anything nice then?" Paul asked Carol. Her and Debbie had spent the day shopping at Maidstone market.

"Not really. A few records, but that's about it."

"It was too cold really and some of the usual stalls didn't turn up," added Debbie. "Tony, can you get me some fags?" she shouted to her boyfriend who was up at the bar talking to Alan.

Back at the table, Tony asked about Bolton. Alan had obviously told him about the poor turnout expected and he wasn't very happy. "If I'm going, Wayne can certainly get off his arse and go and so can Woody and that dipstick Barry. You should have heard the grief I got off the boss today for missing work on Monday - and then I had to ask for Saturday off. He must have thought I was taking the piss."

"I'll give Wayne a ring tomorrow and tell him he's coming whether he likes it or not," said Trev. "I wouldn't count on Woody and Barry though."

"Well, if they can't be arsed travelling, they can leave the Syndicate. It's as simple as that." Tony was obviously in no mood for excuses.

The sound of coins cascading from the fruit machine suddenly attracted everyone's attention. "I've done it! I've fucking done it!" shouted Billy as he began scooping up his winnings. £20 in tokens. Tokens that either had to be fed back into the machine or spent at the bar, but that didn't bother him. "I told you lot and now I've done it!"

"Don't forget to wave when you drive past in your Porsche," commented Big Trev, more for the benefit of those sitting around the table than for Billy's ears.

"Do you fancy a game of pool?" Alan asked Tony.

"Yeah, go on then. You coming Debs?"

The three of them made their way to the pool table, and were soon joined by Trev who saw himself as the skinhead world's answer to Steve Davis. With Bobby studying the tracks on the juke box, that left Paul and Carol alone at the table.

"Are you coming back with me tonight?" asked Paul.

"No, I can't. It's not fair on Debbie's Mum and Dad if I don't go home tonight. Debs told me they weren't too happy when I didn't show up last night. Doesn't mean we can't have some fun before that though."

"Like, what?" asked Paul, his face brightening up again.

"Well, I'm sure we can find somewhere to go. There's a park just across the road isn't there?"

Carol's cheeky smile told Paul he might not have her in his bed tonight, but he would be getting the next best thing. "I tell you what, you go and raid the Durex machine in the gents, and I'll tell Debbie that we're going for a walk." With that, she left Paul sitting at the table, fumbling for a pound coin in his pocket.

When he came out of the toilets, Carol was already waiting for him by the pub entrance. As he walked over to join her, Trev joined Tony in a chorus of "We can see you sneaking out!".

Without turning around, Paul flicked them the V-sign and then escorted Carol out into the night chill.

"Your hands are freezing!" Carol squealed as Paul found his way under her skirt and to the top of her stockings. They continued kissing as Paul started fingering her already wet fanny. The excitement of doing it in the open air in total darkness bar the distant street lights was really turning her on, and Paul's probing was bringing her close to orgasm.

She unbuttoned his sta-press trousers and started massaging him. He was already hard and her stroking quickly made the end of his dick wet with spunk.

Paul was desperate for her and after putting on a johnny, he tried to get inside her. Only with him being a good few inches taller than her and them having to do it standing up, things weren't going to plan like they did in the movies. Paul was beginning to wonder just how Jimmy had banged that bird up the alleyway in *Quadrophenia*.

"Turn around," he said and as she did so he leaned her forward. With one hand holding her knickers over to one side, and the other one guiding his dick into her vagina, they began to make love doggy-style. As he thrust in and out of her, he began fondling her tits and rubbing her clitoris, the combination of which had them both forgetting all about the cold night's air all around them. He came first, but kept pumping, spurred on by her obvious pleasure.

42

A few minutes later and he was buttoning up his trousers and telling her that her shirt was hanging out of the front of her skirt still. Both suitably adjusted, they started to walk back to the pub.

"You'll need to give me your number so that I can give you a ring when you go back," said Paul as he walked along with his arm around Carol.

"I can't," Carol answered. "My Mum would kill me if she thought I had a boyfriend down here. She's really funny when it comes to blokes ringing up. But you could write to me if you wanted."

Paul was not usually one for letter writing, but he was more than willing to make an exception for this young lady. "All right, but you've got to write first, " he said with a smile.

Carol laughed. "Okay then."

"And don't forget to find out about jobs on the boats. As soon as I get a bit of money together, I'll be coming up the M1 like a rocket!"

Back in the pub, the pool table was still attracting everyone's attention. Only Billy was sitting at the table, contemplating how quickly the machine had taken every single token back off him in half an hour flat.

"Have a nice walk over the park did we?" shouted Tony with a smile on his face that went from ear to ear. Even an elbow in the ribs from Debbie didn't wipe it away.

"Yes thank you!" replied Carol with a sarcastic tone in her voice. Paul said nothing, choosing to prop up the bar and wait to be served. He bought a round and took it over to the table. "Feeding time!" he shouted, and slowly but surely the pool table lot made their way back to their seats.

"I think I know where I went wrong," piped up Billy out of the blue.

"Shut up, you plonker!" was Trev's answer to his spark of inspiration. "You've as much chance of beating those machines as I have of shagging Tina Turner so keep it buttoned unless you've something interesting to say."

"No, seriously," said Billy, refusing to be put off. "Anyone got any tens so I can teach it who's boss?"

Everyone just fell about laughing at that one - except Billy of course. Paul was the only one to put his hand in his pocket. "Here you go, mate. Here's ten pence - go and phone all your mates!"

It might have been an old one, but it was enough to start another round of laughs at Billy's expense. Not that it bothered him. He gladly accepted the coin and was back over at the fruit machine before you could say Gambler's Anonymous. "This week the Red Lion, tomorrow Las Vegas!" he boomed as the coin saw him back on his winning streak with a 50p win for three pears.

The rest of them sat around for another twenty minutes and then Debbie announced it was time for her and Carol to call it a night. Tony and Paul put their jackets on, said farewell to the others, and were soon walking the girls home.

As they got to Debbie's front gate, Paul gave Carol a kiss. "I wish you were coming home with me," he whispered.

"So do I, but I'll still see you tomorrow won't I?" Carol leant forward and kissed him again.

"Yeah, four o'clock on the dot."

Paul stood there and watched the best thing that had ever happened to him walk up Debbie's pathway. As the two girls reached the door, they turned and waved goodbye. As he waved back, Paul realised that he didn't give a fuck what his mate's said. His future was definitely in Hull with Carol.

CHAPTER FIVE

PAUL had known Carl Wallis since they were both knee high to a grasshopper. Carl had been a skinhead during 2 Tone's heyday, but had grown out of it long before he'd left school. He didn't even go to football, but Paul still saw his mate as regular as clockwork for a chat and a few beers.

Carl was also the reason why he couldn't meet Carol until four o'clock. He was up in front of the magistrates at West Malling for a breach of the peace offence, following an argument outside a pub in the town two months previous, and Paul had said he'd go along with him for moral support.

The worst thing about West Malling was the distance the station was from the town's centre. All up hill too and by the time they reached the court building there was only minutes to spare.

An official looking old boy told them to take a seat until Carl's case was called, but within seconds, Carl was on his feet again, saying he needed to take a pee. While he was gone, Paul noticed a lady looking over at him. She was in her thirties, smartly dressed and very attractive with it. It must have been that new aftershave, but even if he said so himself, Paul was certainly pulling the birds these days. And without even trying.

He gave her a little smile, wondering whether she was after a bit of rough while her old man was away on business or something. Little did he know that she was just an off-duty policewoman who had to give evidence in the case after Carl's. She thought she recognised

Paul from a shoplifting case from a few months before, and wondered what he'd been up to this time. Getting him into her bed was the last thing on her mind. Still, no point popping the boy's bubble, and he continued to sit there, wondering how he would play it if she made a move.

Carl's return from the bogs soon ended his train of thought. "I hope I don't get too big a fine," Carl said, blocking Paul's view of his bit of skirt.

"No, you'll be okay mate. Just say fuck all, look as if you could burst into tears at any moment and apologise at the end of it all."

There wasn't time for any more last minute nerves. The court doors opened, a few suits came out, and the clerk called for Carl Stephen Wallis to take his place in front of British justice.

As Paul followed the case from his seat in the near empty public gallery, he quickly began to realise that Carl's version of events was wildly different to that of everyone else giving evidence in the case. Carl had told him he had just left a pub after a quiet night's drinking, and had been lifted by two over-zealous young plods looking to boost local arrest statistics.

The first officer who took the stand must have been forty if he was a day. Not exactly the Young Policeman Of The Year candidate described by Carl. And according to his little notepad, he had apprehended the defendant after seeing him attempting to smash a shop window with a metal dustbin that had been ripped from a nearby lamp-post. Only a combination of toughened glass and Carl's drunken state had prevented it going straight through and into an expensive display of china plates.

The old lady who had been walking her dog, the councillor passing in his car and the other police officer all claimed to have seen Carl trying to smash the shop window too. Either they all had a personal grudge against Mr. Wallis or he had been economic with the truth when describing what happened to Paul.

But that wasn't the end of the matter. Apparently Carl had then resisted arrest and had used threatening behaviour towards the two police officers. Following a brief scuffle, he had to be restrained on the ground until a police van arrived with four other officers before he could be carted off to the local cop shop.

Carl listened to the evidence in silence, doing his best to look like he was about to burst into tears at any moment. Mind you, if his acting had been any more wooden, *Eastenders* would have been after him to run the Queen Vic.

When Carl was finally given his chance to speak, he didn't exactly do himself any favours either. "I wasn't doing nothing," he said. "The police just nicked me for no reason. I came out the pub and ended up copping the blame for something some other bastard did."

The old crow of a judge was obviously not impressed by what she saw before her. Carl was wearing jeans, trainers, t-shirt and a hip-length leather jacket. He had also made the mistake of being a young working class male.

"Mr. Wallis, may I remind you that you aren't on the football terraces now and I won't accept bad language in my court room."

"Sorry, your honour," Carl said in a valiant attempt to save the day, "but I've been stitched up by

48

the police. I had only just left the pub when they started picking on me, blaming me for this and that."

"And why would the police want to do that to you?" asked the increasingly impatient magistrate.

"They've just got it in for me. They must have seen me as an easy nick or something. Maybe he's looking for promotion," said Carl, pointing to the forty year old Officer Dibble lookalike.

Paul sat there watching his friend kiss goodbye to any chance he had of being treated leniently. If he'd gone in and pleaded guilty he would have saved everyone a lot of grief. He certainly hadn't been first in the queue to buy that book about how to win friends and influence people.

The magistrate took barely a few minutes to find Carl guilty as charged. "We take a very serious view of public order matters in this courtroom and do not take kindly to bad language and blatantly false stories. If you come before this court again on a similar matter I can assure you that you won't be treated so leniently, but in this instance I'm going to fine you £300."

Carl's acting suddenly improved. A three hundred pound fine was enough to bring tears to any man's eyes. It was certainly a lot of money for bouncing an old dustbin around.

When asked if he had anything to say, Carl kept his mouth shut. He was still trying to take in the size of the fine. Three hundred notes was about twice his expected nightmare scenario. One joker at his work had told him West Malling was a breeze and he'd probably end up with a slapped wrist and a fifty quid lighter wage packet.

"According to the Old Bill, Carl was a one-man riot!" Paul was telling Carol all about his day at court, while they sat in a small cafe just off Gillingham High Street, having something to eat.

"Remind me not to upset him if I ever meet him," Carol said, taking a bite out of her bacon roll.

"Nah, he's usually as good as gold, old Carl. He had just had too much to drink after falling out with his missus. Funny thing was though, he still reckons he was fitted up!"

"What time did you say we'd meet Tony at the station?" asked Carol, realising that time was getting on.

Paul looked at his watch. "Shit, ten minutes ago! Down your coffee and we'll be off."

Within a minute or so, they were leaving the cafe and running along the pedestrianised High Street towards Gillingham station. Paul still had half a cheeseburger in his hand and was doing his best to take bits out of it as they dodged past people heading home after a hard day's work.

It was quarter past six by the time they entered the station and found Tony reading a poster about fare increases for the South-East region.

"About fucking time!" Tony said as Paul and Carol came up to him.

"Sorry we're late, mate," Paul replied. "I've been at court all day with Carl, and lost track of time in the cafe."

Tony wasn't that bothered really. If the truth be known he had arrived ten minutes late himself. "So how did he get on then?"

"Three hundred note fine!"

"Fuck me!" said Tony, surprised by the size of it. "Three hundred pounds for breach of the peace?"

"Yeah that, and all the other offences Carl conveniently forgot to tell us about!"

Tony had parked his car just up the road from the station, and it was only a fifteen minute drive to Debbie's house in Strood, on the other side the River Medway. Her parents went to bingo every Wednesday night, so she had invited Tony and Paul to join her and Carol for a night in.

A video and a few cans of beer were on the menu, and no sooner had they arrived when Debbie sent the two blokes off to the local corner shop to get them.

While they were out getting the supplies, Debbie and Carol were in the kitchen, making Tony something for his tea. He had met Carol and Paul straight from work, and hadn't stopped complaining about his empty belly since seeing Paul pop the last piece of cheeseburger into his mouth.

"So what did you get up to this afternoon then?" Debbie asked her friend as she put some sausages under the grill.

"Not much, really. Just had a quick look around Gillingham and then went and got something to eat."

"No looking in jeweller's shop windows I hope?" said Debbie, looking at Carol with a disapproving eye.

"No way!" said Carol, laughing it off. "Me and Paul are just having fun. Once I'm back in Hull, it'll be all finished with and the only wedding rings I'll be looking at will be mine and Ray's."

"And you've told him about Ray I suppose?"

"Of course not," replied Carol as she buttered some bread. "What's the point?"

"The point is, I think Paul has fallen for you hook, line and sinker, and he's too nice a bloke to get hurt."

Carol was beginning to get annoyed by Debbie shoving her nose in where it wasn't wanted. She was worse than her Mum and that was saying something. As far as Carol was concerned, she was just letting her hair down for a final time before getting married to Ray that summer. "Look, I'm going home tomorrow. I've had a great time and so has Paul, so let's just leave it at that, eh?"

"Yeah, okay," Debbie said, deciding to drop the subject. All the same she wasn't looking forward to picking up the pieces once Carol was back in Hull. Especially if Paul thought Debbie and Tony should have told him that Carol was spoken for and was just after a good time while down south.

"That film was crap," said Tony, as Debbie ushered him and Paul out of the house minutes before her parents were due back from their traditional drink after a night out at the bingo.

"How do you know?" Debbie replied, "you were snoring through most of it!"

"Yeah, well. Just shows how shit it was," Tony replied as he dug his car keys out of his jacket pocket.

Carol gave Paul a quick goodnight kiss and said she would see him in the morning.

"I'll come around about half-eleven, okay," Paul called, as he waited for Tony to unlock the passenger door. "That'll give us plenty of time to get to the station."

"Safe journey home, Carol," said Tony as he got into his car, knowing he wouldn't see Carol again before she headed back to Hull.

"Yeah, thanks for everything, Tony, and see you again soon!" Carol called back from the doorstep of the small terrace house.

With the front door closed, the two girls went back into the living room to clear away the empty beer cans. She didn't say anything, but Debbie was all too aware when Tony would see Carol next. When they travelled up to Hull for her wedding.

CHAPTER SIX

AS he got off the bus, Paul dug his hands deep into his sheepskin pockets to keep warm. He looked up at the tower block he called home and wished he'd got on the train back to Hull with Carol.

Instead he was left to walk the short distance across the green wasteland that stood between his block of flats and the road. As he pushed the main door open, he noticed the shabby collection of scruffs hanging about in the ground floor lobby. If one of them hadn't spoken, he might have walked past, thinking they were a pile of dustbin sacks waiting to be collected.

"Watch out. Here comes action man," the voice said as Paul headed for the stairs.

"Someone talking to me?" Paul asked as he turned to face the low life that polluted his estate. He had just said goodbye to the new love of his life and the last thing he needed was some joker noising him up.

There was silence as Paul stood facing his taunters. Then one of them piped up. "Watch out kids - he might tell his old Mum on us."

The bloke doing the talking was one of the people who lived in the flat above him. He was a skinny looking bloke with unkempt hair and a week's growth of beard. From his tone of voice and the smiles on the other faces, Paul took his last comment to mean that they had been noising up his Mum in some way.

"What's she got to do with it?" Paul asked, looking directly at the scruffy bastard doing all the talking.

"Nothing," came the weasly reply. "We just wouldn't want anything to happen to her when you're not about that's all."

Paul had taken enough shit and didn't take kindly to scum of the earth threatening his Mum. He went to grab the bastard by the collar to nut him, but backed off when his tormentor suddenly pulled out a needle and waved it in his face.

"Careful, action man. You wouldn't want to hurt yourself would you? After all, I might have AIDS!"

Before Paul could react, two of the others in the group had produced knives and were pointing them menacingly in his direction. "You're fucking scum, you lot," he said angrily, as he began to move away towards the stairs.

"That's it," said the bloke waving the needle. "Hurry home to see if Mummy is okay!"

Paul turned and ran up the stairs as fast as his legs would carry him. As laughter echoed around the stairwell from down below, he was convinced they had done something to his Mum. He reached his flat on the fifth floor, gasping for air, and fumbled to unlock the door.

As he entered the flat, he could smell something cooking in the kitchen at the other end of the hall. Then the kitchen door opened, and his Mum said, "You're just in time for your tea, Paul. Go and wash your hands and I'll serve up."

Thank God! Paul thought, as he went into the bathroom to wash his hands and face, his heart still racing. Nothing had happened to his Mum, but he was still going to make those bastards pay for digging him up. And if they ever said so much as "Boo!" to his Mum, he would have every single one of the them.

There was never anything on TV on a Friday night, and Paul spent most of the evening in his room, sorting out his records and thinking about Carol. She would be more or less home by now and here he was stuck in a fucking box half way up a concrete tower, hundreds of miles away. Life was a bitch, it really was.

Tomorrow he was helping out Alan and his Dad on their stall at Rochester market which would give him the money for football the day after, but come Monday he was going to get himself a decent job no matter what. He didn't care what he had to do to get the money to move up to Hull. If the stuck-up bitch in the Jobcentre offered him a job cleaning toilets, he was going to take it. Anything to be with Carol.

Paul had had plenty of birds before, and he was the first to admit that he got too involved with some of them far too quickly. It usually ended in tears, and mostly his, but Carol was a totally different ball game. He had never wanted to be with a girl as much as he did this one. What they had between them was something special.

It was obvious she felt the same way about him. He had only know her a few days, and she was crying buckets for fuck's sake as her train pulled away earlier that afternoon. And when they had made love in his room that night, Carol had almost consumed him with her passion.

He shoved an album from his *Tighten Up* box set on to his turntable, and lay back on his bed, listening to

Joya Landis singing *Angel Of The Morning* and thinking of his angel of a few nights before. The memory of her on top of him, naked, moving up and down as he handled her tits and kissed them, was enough to give him an instant erection. Christ, what he'd give to have her in his room now, or over the park, or even in the cinema in Folkestone. Even a re-run of this morning at Debbie's house would be Paul's idea of heaven.

He had arrived at about twenty past eleven to find Carol in the house alone. Debbie and her parents were out at work, and the taxi to the train station had been booked for midday. That left them half an hour alone, and as soon as he'd walked through the front door, Carol had left him in no doubt what she wanted.

They had kissed and fondled in the hall, before Carol had led him through to the front room. There, she allowed his hands to go up her skirt, feeling her arse and her fanny as they did so. She was busy herself, undoing his jeans so that she could free his dick. Then they had gone over to the settee, and with her sitting on the edge and Paul kneeling down, they had made love. Something the old settee was used to if Tony's stories about late night sessions while Debbie's parents were in bed were anything to go by.

His Mum knocking on his door interrupted his thoughts. "I'm off to bed Paul, good night."

"Yeah, night Mum!"

Getting up off his bed, he went over to his record player and turned down the music. Then moving over to his window sill, he picked up a pen and notepad. He knew he had told Carol to write first, but couldn't wait to tell this girl how much she meant to him. And if he couldn't see her in the flesh or talk to her on the 'phone, then he would have to rely on good old Royal Mail to reach her heart.

Writing down his thoughts didn't come naturally to Paul, but he did his best to let her know how much he'd enjoyed being with her and how he was determined to get up to Hull as soon as possible. As he wrote, he had a horrible feeling in his stomach, a feeling any person will know if they've been separated from a loved one for any length of time. A sort of mixture between aching for their company and a nagging belief that they might be having the time of their lives while you were out of sight, out of mind.

He surprised himself by filling six pages and closed by telling her to write soon. As he sealed the envelope, he wondered if he'd come over too heavy, but decided he hadn't. Some people were made for each other, and he knew that was the case with him and Carol. And if he didn't tell her exactly how he felt, how the fuck would she ever know?

* * *

Tony was just getting into the bath when his brother had shouted up the stairs that Debbie was on the 'phone. Pulling a towel around his waist, he unlocked the door and went down to talk to her. "Alright, Debs."

"Yeah, I'm fine. That's Carol just phoned to say she got back okay."

"Good," he replied. He knew exactly what was coming next too.

"So are you going to tell Paul about her being engaged to be married?"

"Course I ain't! I told you before, he'll soon forget about her once some other bird comes along, you just wait and see!"

Debbie obviously wasn't so sure. Somehow she felt responsible for all of Tony's mates, making sure they all got home after a night on the tiles, that sort of thing. And she felt especially concerned for Paul because it was her who had introduced him to Carol without mentioning she was spoken for. "And that's why he was telling Billy and Alan he was thinking of moving to Hull was it?"

"Look, that's just talk. Paul wouldn't leave the Medway Towns. He had a good time with Carol and that'll be it."

"Well, just remember who he's going to blame if he gets hurt," Debbie said, pouring on the emotional pressure. "He's not going to be too pleased when he finds out his best friend wasn't looking out for him."

"Okay, okay," said Tony, giving in to his better half. "I'll have a word with him at football on Saturday and see what he says. Now, is there any chance of me having my bath now?"

"Oh, no!" screamed Debbie with mock hysteria. "Don't tell me I forgot your birthday!"

"Very funny, Debbie. Now piss off and let me have me bath in peace."

"Okay, babe. Nighty-night. And don't let the bed bugs bite!"

Tony said goodnight and put the receiver down. As he walked back up the stairs, he was thinking about Paul and Carol. And especially Carol. Tony had ended

59

up giving her one on Debbie's settee the last time she was down from Hull for a weekend.

All three of them had spent a warm Saturday afternoon drinking, Debbie had gone upstairs to lay down because she was feeling a bit sick, and with Debbie's parents out for the day, one thing had led to another. It was all over in a matter of minutes, and had never been mentioned since. Which was just as well really, because if Debbie ever found out he'd be dead meat.

One thing was for sure. He knew exactly what Paul was missing out on now that Carol was back in Hull. Even at sixteen, inexperienced she wasn't, and less than a year on he was certain she'd have given Paul value for his money.

Rochester market was always busy. Its tightly packed stalls meant you could hardly move come eleven o'clock. Alan's father had a stall at the top end of the market, selling mainly leather jackets and coats. Paul had actually bought his first crombie off this stall before he had even met Alan. Fourteen quid it had cost him, a bargain at twice the price.

"Did you hear about Woody?" Alan said as he returned from the catering van with cups of tea for his old man, himself and Paul.

"No, I ain't seen him for ages," replied Paul.

"No wonder. He only sent photos of his bird into *Knave* for the readers' wives page!"

"Don't tell me they printed them," said Paul, grinning as he shook his head.

"Too right they did. Funny thing is though, the first Sally knew about it was when her old boy opened his copy and saw his daughter standing there with her tits out!"

"For fuck's sake!" Paul exclaimed. "Her Dad'll fuckin' murder Woody if he gets hold of him. And I bet Sally ain't too pleased with him either!"

By now Alan was helping a customer try on a full-length black leather coat, but it didn't stop him chatting away. "That's why we ain't seen Woody. He's gone into hiding! He was on the phone to me and all he could say was, 'Still, I got twenty quid for it'!"

"That kid's a bloody idiot," Alan's Dad said, as he went to the other end of the stall to see if he could do some business with a young lady looking at the suede jackets. "Best on the market, love!" he called out as he headed towards her.

"I better pick up a copy on my way home to see what all the fuss is about!" Paul joked, as Alan pocketed the thirty-five quid from the sale.

"Well, Sally is a big girl so you won't be disappointed!"

"Oi! Paul," Alan's Dad shouted over, "Go into the back of the van and see if we've got any black suede jackets, size 12!"

"Yeah, no problem," Paul replied, knowing that a size 14 on a coat hanger labelled size 12 would do just as well if they didn't. The trick in this game was whatever size the customer asked for, was the one you had on the van.

CHAPTER SEVEN

BY the time the boys had changed trains at Manchester and waited for their connection, time was getting on. They arrived at Bolton station just before three o'clock, and after getting directions off an old boy in the street outside, they made their way to the ground.

Luckily it was a 3.15 kick-off and they arrived at the turnstiles with a few minutes to spare. In the end, and thanks to a lot of arm-twisting from Tony, eight Syndicate members had made the trip. Tony, Paul, Big Trev, Alan, Billy, Bobby, Wayne, and Simon, who had decided to go whether his father liked it or not. And they looked the part too, all dressed in jeans, green flight jackets and cherry red DM boots.

Bolton Wanderers were once one of the biggest names in English football and their big ground showed traces of their former glory. But now the club languished in the Third Division, the crowds had dwindled, and the team they now sent out on a Saturday afternoon showed little sign of bringing back the good times. In fact there was every chance that the Gills would go home with at least a point from this fixture, and probably all three like they did last season.

Gillingham fans had been allocated just a corner of the ground, which meant the latecomers had to walk the length of a deserted terrace, populated by just one or two bobbies, to reach it.

As the skinheads made their way across the terracing they were like sitting ducks to the noise merchants in the home end. Chants of "Who the fucking hell are you?" were quickly followed by "You're going home in a Lancashire ambulance!"

"Very original!" Billy shouted back at the top of his voice, but they wouldn't have heard him. The 300 or so Gillingham fans already in the cramped corner made up for it though with chants of "Wankashire! La-la-la! Wankashire! La-la-la!"

By the time the skinheads had made their way to the heart of the Gillingham support, Big Trev had started off another barrage of chanting. "Ooh-aah, ooh to be, ooh to be a Southerner!" were the words being hurled over the fence in the direction of the great unwashed of Bolton.

The first-half was pretty mediocre - not that you expected Brazilian skills in the Third. Most of the excitement had been generated on the terraces, with Bolton's fifty strong younger mob baying at the Gillingham fans through the fence and the Gills faithful hurling abuse back at them, with a favourite taunts being "Back to school, boys!" and "Have you seen a ten pound note!", accompanied by the waving of banknotes just to rub it in.

"Fancy a pie?" Paul asked Tony as the ref blew for half-time, and with a nodded reply they both made their way to the tiny stall selling out of date Wagon Wheels and the like. As it happened the pies had sold out before their turn came, which was probably just as well judging by the complaints about them being cold in the middle from those who had been unfortunate enough to pay good money for them.

Mind you, eating anything from an away end stall was dodgy to say the least. Paul knew a bloke who ritually pissed into the tea urn at a certain dog track before every meeting, so you could imagine what the likes of pasties and Bovril go through at away ends up and down the country.

As they walked back to their mates with a Mars bar each, Tony asked Paul if he was going to see Carol again.

"Yeah, if all goes to plan. I'm going to see if I can get some work up her way and see how it goes from there."

"If I was you, mate, I'd forget all about her. Get yourself a nice bit of southern skirt."

It was said half-jokingly, but Paul sensed that Tony knew something he didn't. "Why do you say that?" he said.

"No reason really," answered Tony. "I just don't think you should throw your life away on a bird you hardly know, that's all."

The subject was dropped, but it left a nagging feeling in the back of Paul's mind that maybe Debbie had said something. Or maybe it was just Tony, not wanting to see a good mate disappear up north, never to be seen again. God knows he had enough trouble trying to hold the mob together without them disappearing at the first sign of a bit of the other.

Ten minutes into the second half and Gillingham went a goal up. Bolton managed to equalise, but minutes later the Gills were in front again thanks to a Dave Shearer header. He had only been at the club since July, but was already a firm favourite with the Gillingham fans.

It was enough to win them the game and for the last half hour the Gillingham end celebrated another three points towards promotion. Bolton's performance was well below par for a home team and their fans vented their anger and disappointment at the party animals over in the corner. Chants of "You're gonna get your fucking heads kicked in!" echoed around Burnden Park.

Come the final whistle, Gillingham's jubilant support was kept behind to allow the home fans to disperse. Or to take up their battle positions as the case may be. When the gates were finally opened, mounted policemen greeted the Gills fans, but only escorted them the length of the away end and on to the main road. Then they abandoned the Gillingham fans to find their own way home.

The MSS had joined up with about 25 other lads who were looking for a bit of aggro before heading for the train. And they didn't take long to find it either. Just three hundred yards from the ground, about 30 Bolton under-fives came out of a side street and charged the Gillingham fans.

The Gillingham mob stood its ground with ease and were soon furiously fighting away with the Wanderers fans. Running battles across the main road were interrupted only by respect for the damage the passing cars could do. Even so, one young Bolton casual got knocked over and was soon set upon by four or five Gillingham fans, including Wayne. Elsewhere fists and feet were flying, as the rival mobs fought for control of the street.

Then half a dozen motors came racing down the same side street and emptied their human contents into the thick of the action. These boys were bigger and older, and obviously Bolton's top lads. Some carried pickaxe handles, others baseball bats, as they started to turn the tide against those trespassing on their turf.

Paul, Big Trev and Alan were standing together when two of the weapon-wielding arrivals charged into them. A baseball bat caught Trevor smack in the face despite his vain attempts to stop it with his arms. If Alan hadn't backed him up at that crucial moment he would no doubt have ended up in hospital. Paul had managed to avoid the flailing half snooker cue being waved in front of him, and had even managed to force the bastard back before the sound of sirens speeding towards the battling youths ended the party.

By the time the plods had arrived it was all over. Only the odd abandoned weapon and the state of some of the Gillingham fans provided any evidence that a public order offence had been committed. One of the Gillingham fans was wandering around aimlessly, his ski-jacket ripped to shreds and his nose bleeding badly. He had obviously taken a severe kicking, but apart from Trev, the MSS had come out of the ruck relatively unharmed.

Everyone was buzzing as they made their way further down the road. Amazingly the police made no effort to provide an escort for the Gillingham rowdies and once again left them to fend for themselves.

With the adrenaline flowing, everyone wanted more action. As they walked through a bus station, Tony produced a tin of aerosol paint spray from his jacket pocket, and wrote MSS - WE ARE FUCKING EVERYWHERE! in foot high letters on the wall beneath the timetables. As he did so, a shout went up as some Gillingham fans spotted some Bolton casuals on the top deck of a stationary bus.

A dozen or more steamed on to it, much to the horror of the ordinary passengers, and charged up the stairs. There were only five casuals to be found and they took a severe hiding off the invaders. Within fifteen or twenty seconds it was all over, and as proof of their victory, one of the casuals was dragged screaming and kicking down the stairs and given another beating outside. Big Trev was straight over to put the boot in as pay back for his aching face.

Scared shoppers just looked on helplessly, as the poor kid was kicked senseless. Other Gillingham fans were now rampaging all over the bus station, looking for Bolton fans to punish. Even scarfers were getting hit for being in the wrong place at the right time.

Alan, meanwhile, had found two scruffy bastards who had obviously been selling *Socialist Worker* to the good people of Bolton. Judging by the number of copies they were still carrying, they hadn't found many buyers either.

"What do you mean, troops out?" demanded Alan, as he pointed to the front page headline. "Troops out of where?"

"Troops out of Ireland," came the reply.

"You people make me sick with your fucking student politics!" Alan said, giving the biggest one a slap around the head. "Socialist worker? Your sort don't know what working is, let alone socialism! Fucking middle class tosser!"

"Leave him alone you fascist bastard!" screamed the little one. From her appearance you would never have guessed it was a girl, but her voice gave the game away.

"Who you calling a fascist?" said Paul, as the rest of the MSS descended on the hapless newspaper sellers. He grabbed at the bloke's 'papers and threw them into the air. "Who's a fucking fascist?" he screamed, his face now about an inch away from the bigger socialist worker.

"All skinheads are fascist. And if you're not a fascist, you shouldn't dress up as one." You had to hand it to him, the bloke had bottle. Either that or he was heavily under the influence of glue.

"Fuck you dickhead! What do you know about skinheads? What do you know about anything? Fucking textbook communists, that's all you cunts are."

"Communism isn't . . . " The wannabe revolutionary didn't have time to finish his sentence. Paul nutted him in the face, knocking him backwards.

"Don't give me any of your bullshit, you useless piece of shit!" Paul shouted as the female Socialist Worker screamed at him to leave her partner alone.

Paul turned to walk away, kicking at the 'papers now littering the floor. The other skinheads followed behind him, leaving Simon to add insult to injury. "If you had a bath love I might be interested in giving you one!"

"When your balls drop I'll let my dog know!" she shouted as she started to pick up the scattered newspapers.

A jobsworth had obviously called the police because the Medway skinheads hadn't even left the bus station when two riot vans pulled up. By now the other Gillingham fans were well away from the scene, and so the police's attention naturally focused on the strangers with shaven heads.

"What are you up to then, lads?" asked a police officer with a couple of stripes on the arm of his jacket. Big bloke he was too.

"Nothing sir," said Big Trev with all the conviction of a choirboy. "We were looking for the train station."

"Well, you won't find it here will you," the burly officer replied.

The Syndicate had finally found themselves an escort out of town, and for the five minute stroll to Bolton railway station, they were accompanied by three PCs and a policewoman. Just as well really because this thin blue line was all that was keeping at bay the 50 strong Bolton mob that was hanging around the road junction that led to the station. Paul gave them a wave as he turned the corner, and that was the last they would see of Bolton for another season at least.

Once on the train, the MSS soon found the other Gillingham hooligans occupying the best part of a smoking carriage. Some of the boys had found a couple of birds to chat up, and even the bloke who had been wandering around like a random motion machine after the first bit of trouble had perked up enough to join in the singing.

Big Trev's left eye was coming up a treat. He would need a bloody big steak to take that swelling away, and Alan's joke offering of the beefburger he had bought at the station cafe was met with the derision it deserved. "Fuck off, you cheeky bastard!"

The train was soon on its way through the Lancashire countryside and heading for Manchester. Then it was a quick dash over the bridge to another platform, and the boys were on an Inter-City to London which to everyone's delight had a buffet car.

While stocking up on cans of beer, Billy stumbled upon a couple of skinheads from Luton who had been working in Blackpool, and he brought them back to where the others were sitting for the usual chat about music, birds and football.

The journey south passed quickly thanks to the flowing ale and in next to no time the train was pulling into Luton. The two skinheads said their farewells to the Gillingham boys and promised to keep in touch. A few tins and a couple of hands at cards later, and the train had arrived at Euston station.

Euston was well-known as a warzone for rival mobs. So many different supporters passed through it on a Saturday, either on their way to games in the capital or games up north, that it was inevitable that there would be trouble. Inside the station wasn't the place to kick things off though due to the presence of security cameras, but the streets around Euston had seen many a battle in their day.

The MSS had no time to hang about tonight however. Two taxis were summoned to cart them across the city to Charing Cross to catch the train to the Medway Towns that would get them back before closing time. Lady Luck had obviously taken the day off though and they missed it by a matter of minutes.

"Oh well, might as well find a boozer," said Tony after seeing that the next train home didn't leave until twenty past midnight.

"That'll do me," enthused Billy, with visions of a new fruit machine to conquer.

It wasn't hard finding a pub. A little street just off Charing Cross Road offered a choice of two and the boys chose the first one they came to.

"Six pints of lager and two pints of bitter please guv," shouted Tony as he tried to attract the attention of the landlord. The bloke behind the bar was in his forties, was overweight and balding, but he looked like he could still handle himself.

"I'll serve you and your mates, but I'm not serving him," the publican said, pointing a fat finger in the direction of young Simon.

The poor kid's face turned bright red with embarrassment, and the others didn't help matters with comments about bed-time and the like. Still, at least he had a couple of cans to keep him warm as he took his leave and waited outside for his mates.

Paul picked up a pint of lager and a pint of bitter, and walked over to Billy who was in his element with a choice of two machines. "Having any joy?" he asked.

"I'm trying out a system that bloke Dave from Luton told me about. It's all on the nudges." Billy hadn't even turned around. His eyes were too busy working out fruit permutations.

"Here, I'll put your pint up here," said Paul, not wanting to disturb the master at work. "Give me a shout if you win anything." And with that he walked back to the others who had found themselves a window seat. A low curtain on a rail prevented the passing public looking into the pub, but both Big Trev and Alan were kneeling on the seat so that they could look out at Simon shivering away with his can of lager. Just to rub it in, both were blowing into cupped hands, as if they were keeping warm themselves.

"Leave the kid alone," Paul said. "I tell you what, he handled himself well today."

Alan turned around from looking out the window. "Yeah, I know. I saw him give some casual a kick in the balls that he won't forget in a hurry."

"The little bastard is even getting his end away with that bird he sometimes knocks about with," said Wayne. "You know, the fat slag in the school uniform."

"Who told you that then?" asked Paul.

"He told me himself", Wayne explained inbetween gulps of lager. "Reckons all he had to do was tell her he loved her and she was letting him do all sorts."

"Yeah, in his fucking dreams," said a dismissive Big Trev who just couldn't accept that the little runt was enjoying the good things in life when the nearest he'd come to a screw in the last six months was visiting his brother in Ashford nick. "When I was his age I was lucky to get a handful of tit."

"That's more than you've been getting lately my son!" joked Wayne with a laugh.

It wasn't that Trev was particularly ugly or had a bad case of body odour. It was simply that his social world revolved around football and getting bevvied with his mates, and neither provided a perfect setting for bird-pulling. Even dances and gigs usually had the blokes outnumbering the girls five to one.

* * *

Leroy and Mark were Arsenal supporters. They had watched the gang of skinheads coming into the pub from their small round table over in the corner by the toilets. And what they saw were the dregs of society. Working class Neanderthals who inhabited concrete jungles in ever-decreasing numbers. Like the dodo, they were becoming extinct.

Leroy in particular hated the bastards with the little brains and the big boots. As a fourteen year old he had been beaten up by a gang of Chelsea skinheads because of the colour of his skin. Black. That's all they knew about him and that's all they wanted to know. What made it worse was that the attack happened during the rush hour in a passage connecting Underground tube platforms, and not one of the countless passing faces tried to help him. Not even the black London Transport employee, who pretended he hadn't seen anything so that he didn't have to get involved.

Mark was white and had nothing against skinheads in general. Some of his best mates at school had been skins as had his two older brothers. As he was fond of saying, he held no prejudices. He saw everyone as fair game for a slapping if he thought they deserved it. Blacks, whites, pakis, chinks, aliens from out of space even. And tonight, he was as certain as Leroy that someone would deserve it, whether it was the buffoon at the fruit machines or one of the other arseholes acting like six year olds over by the window.

* * *

The pub served a decent pint which made the high London prices a little easier to swallow. There was nothing worse than paying over the odds for piss-poor beer. Alas all good things must come to an end, and after their second round was near completion, Tony gestured that it was time to be off.

"I need a slash, so I'll catch you outside," said Paul before heading for the bogs.

"Shake it more than three times and you're wanking!" bellowed Trev 's voice just before Paul reached the door marked gents.

As he went in, Paul didn't notice the two blokes sitting by the door get up and follow in his foot steps. Even when he was pissing into one of the three urinals, the sound of another person or persons in the toilets didn't give him cause to worry.

Careful only to shake his dick twice, Paul zipped up his trousers and turned to make his way back into the hustle and bustle of the pub. "Alright mate," he said, as he passed the black guy standing by the door, who was evidently waiting for his mate who was over by the sink. But everything wasn't all right.

Just as Paul went to pull open the door leading back into the pub, Leroy pulled an empty beer bottle from inside his jacket and smashed it over Paul's head with enough force for it to smash on impact. Paul fell forward, crashing against the door. Before he could steady himself, both Leroy and Mark were booting fuck out of him. Paul tried to curl up in a ball, his arms cradling his face in an attempt to stop the blows, but before any time at all he was just a crumpled mess lying on the toilet floor. The alcohol consumed during the day was helping to numb the pain, but even in his half-conscious state Paul could taste the blood and vomit that he was coughing up.

* * *

After leaving the fruit machines, Billy decided he'd take a pee too before joining the others outside. It wasn't until he tried to push the door open that he heard the sound of fighting above the noise of a pub full of rowdy drinkers and a blaring juke box.

Someone was obviously getting the shit kicked out of him just the other side of the toilet door. Billy froze for a moment, then turned away. He didn't want to get involved. Didn't want to risk getting it himself. Instead, he turned and headed into the street to join the others - without saying a word about what he'd heard.

* * *

Knowing that at least one person must have known something was up, Leroy decided to bid farewell to the unconscious skinhead. Reaching into his inside jacket pocket, he took out a small CS gas can. He then turned the skinhead's face towards him, propped open his eyes with his fingers and sprayed some of the contents of the can directly into them. Paul writhed and screamed in pain as his burning eyes brought him back to his senses.

"Hope that blinds you, you fucking bastard!"

* * *

Outside the pub, the conversation had moved on to sunnier climbs. With little else to do, Simon had spent the last half hour looking at the cards in the travel agent window directly opposite the pub. And now he

75

was teasing the others with tales of holidays to Jamaica for only £349.

"Yeah, but you wouldn't be able to go to Orange Street or Prince Buster's shop," complained Alan. "It's in the middle of a ghetto and you'd get your head cut off quicker than you could say Red Stripe!"

"Surely Prince Buster isn't still there is he?" asked Tony, certain that the ska legend wouldn't be standing behind a shop counter twenty years on selling mint copies of *Al Capone*.

Before he could get an answer, the pub doors opened and everyone turned expecting to see Paul. Instead two blokes stood there, solid-looking lads, one black one white. "I don't want to worry you," said the black one, as he passed Big Trev. "But I think one of your mates is being sick in the toilet."

Trev let out a laugh. "Never could hold his drink that one! Cheers mate, I'll go and see how he's doing!"

"No problem," said the darkie as he joined his mate and headed off towards the bright lights of Regent Street.

At first, Trev couldn't open the toilet door. Something was blocking it from the inside. He was about to call the landlord when he heard someone moaning and coughing. He tried again and this time managed to get his head around the door. He looked down and saw Paul lying there, all curled up in a ball, spewing his guts. The shattered glass all around him, and the blood coming from the back of his head and face, told Trev immediately that it wasn't just the drink that had taken its toll.

Pushing the door open, Trev squeezed through and crouched down by Paul.

"What happened?" he said, trying to bring Paul back into the land of the conscious as he spoke. "Who did this to you? Was it that black bastard and his white mate?"

Paul could hear Trev's voice and was glad to know that the cavalry had arrived, but he was in no fit state for explanations. He wasn't even sure what had happened himself. All he knew was that he wanted to get out of the toilet and into the fresh air.

Paul's eyes were streaming from the effects of the CS gas, but at least he could still see. The burning sensation was easing, but the rest of his body was a mess of bloody cuts and pain.

Trev saw that his mate was trying to stand and helped him to his feet. "Come on, blue," he said. "Let's get you home."

CHAPTER EIGHT

NEARLY a week had passed since the Bolton game and Paul was almost back on top form. Even so, he had to miss Tuesday's session down the pub. True to his word, he had gone out on Monday looking for a job and had come up trumps with a full-time job, filling shelves on the nightshift at the new Saveshop supermarket on the outskirts of Gillingham.

It wasn't the best of jobs, stacking tins of fruit and packets of icing sugar, but it would put money in his pocket at the end of every week. And once he had put enough by, it would be his passport to Hull and Carol. Something he wanted even more after what had happened to him on Saturday.

Working across the aisle from him was one of his old schoolmates, Tommy Peters. He hadn't seen Tommy for six or seven years, and come the half-hour meal break, they had a lot of catching up to do.

"What the fuck were you doing in London anyway?" asked Tommy as his friend complained about the weight of some of the boxes causing his aching ribs some serious grief.

"It's a long story mate, but I was on my way back from the football."

"Don't tell me you're still involved in football violence?" asked Tommy with disbelief written all over his face. "I thought you would have grown out of that phase by now!"

Paul had first got involved with football mobs when he was fifteen, and as a fifth-former had already developed quite a reputation as an aggro merchant.

Paul remembered Tommy was as impressed as the others back then, but the passing of time had obviously taken the shine off things.

It was okay for the likes of Tommy though. He didn't even go to matches. He claimed to support Manchester United, but all that amounted to was watching them two or three times a season on *Match Of The Day*. Hardly number one fan material.

To Paul, football violence wasn't something you could just walk away from. Not unless you had a magic ticket to the executive boxes or wanted to fork out for a seat in the stand with the granddads and the halfwits. If you stood at an end, giving vocal support to your club, then like it or not, football violence would come looking for you. A mob following the away team would turn up at your end of the ground and try to take it. You could either run away and let them. Or you could make a stand. And as far as Paul was concerned, there was no alternative to taking them on.

"Maybe if a few more people supported their local team, nobody would try it on and we wouldn't need to fight," said Paul, having a dig at Tommy and the thousands of others who turned their back on Gillingham in favour of some distant team that they owed no loyalty to that you could put your finger on.

"Sorry Paul, but I don't see how fighting with other fans does Gillingham or football any good at all. No wonder gates are at an all-time low."

"So what am I supposed to do then? Shake hands with some bastard who tries to take the Rainham End and buy him a pint after he's kicked my head in? We're talking real world here, not Jimmy Hill."

Tommy wasn't convinced. "So what happens if the next bloke you thump dies from his injuries. What would you do then? Put that down to defending the good name of Gillingham?"

Three or four years ago, Paul would probably have answered yes and not given a fuck. But the older he got, the more he realised the damage he could inflict on another human being. And more to the point, the damage others could cause to him, especially with the increasing use of weapons at and around football games. If he could walk away, he probably would have done, but it wasn't as simple as that. His life revolved around following Gillingham, and if rival fans wanted to mix it, he wasn't going to stand by and watch his mates take a good hiding.

"Smoking kills too," Paul said, pointing to the fag hanging out of Tommy's mouth. He knew fine well he was dodging the issue, but at three in the morning he just wasn't in the mood to argue the toss.

"Fancy a drink?" Tommy asked as he got up from the table and walked over to the soft drinks machine.

"A can of beer would do nicely!"

"I'm sure it would Mr. West. But you'll have to wait until you leave here to satisfy your thirst." The voice coming from behind him was that of the night manager, Steven Reid. It was Reid who had given Paul the job and for a boss he was not a bad bloke to work for.

"Only joking, Mr. Reid. Believe me, the last thing I want now is a can of beer," Paul replied, his mind flashing back to the foul cocktail of beer, sick and blood that had filled his mouth a week or so before.

"Good to hear it. Now is there any chance of those fruit shelves being filled by eight o'clock? I don't want to rush you, but we would like to let the public in sometime tomorrow. Preferably in the morning."

With those words of sarcasm, Steven Reid turned to address the others sitting in the staff canteen. "Okay, boys and girls. Let's get back out there and get the job done." And as people started to get to their feet and make their way back to work, he added for the benefit of *Hill Street Blues* fans, "And remember, be careful out there."

With his aisle completed, Paul headed for the warehouse where all the stock was kept. Out on the shop floor, the night manager and his henchmen could keep a close eye on whether you were working or not, but it was amazing the time you could waste pissing about in the warehouse. It was almost as good as the walk-in freezer where nobody ever went without the thermal clothing needed to stop you turning into a giant ice pole.

Paul had only worked there a couple of days, and already he'd been amazed by what went on in that warehouse. On his first night, he'd been sent there to sweep up and had stumbled across the young kid who did the washing powder shagging one of the married thirty-something women from diary products. Then there was Dwayne, a bloke in his twenties, who was in there every half hour eating his way through a packet of biscuits or a few bars of chocolate.

It was also the easiest way to get knock-off food and other goods out of the store. All you had to do was get what you wanted from the warehouse shelves and pass it under the gates or over the wall in the delivery yard to a waiting mate. Two of the blokes were supplying a market trader with enough tinned fruit every week to feed an army. And the Chinese army at that.

If Paul was to make it to Hull in double quick time, then he'd have to get involved in some of the fiddles. Tonight though, all that he found to put a smile on his dial was a couple of blokes dropping cartons of eggs on to the floor.

"What the fuck are you two up to?" he asked.

"Oh, some bastard hasn't been rotating the stock and so the day shift has been taking fresh eggs from the front," said the older of the two men. "These ones at the back have been out of date for weeks, and the boss wants us to get rid of them before the day manager arrives and blames us for the cock-up."

"After all," added the other man, "accidents will happen!" And with that he sent another box containing nearly three hundred eggs crashing to the floor. Talking to Paul, he then said, "Tell you what. You give Arthur a hand with this and I'll go and get the mops so we can get this little lot cleaned up."

Paul just laughed and joined in the fun. It would have been easier just shoving the boxes straight into the waste skips, but then again they had the time to kill and so might as well have some fun . . .

That night, Paul thought that working there might be a lot better than he'd imagined, but by the following Friday he was brought back to Earth with an almighty bump. He turned up for the night shift at ten o'clock as usual, only to find that he was out of a job. The store manager had sacked half the night crew, including the union rep, and Paul's name was on the list of losers.

Most of those sacked were young men, regardless of whether they were doing a good job or not. In fact, two of the old cows who had kept their jobs were so lazy everyone called them the walking dead. Obviously, someone had found out about all the stuff going missing and had decided to sack everyone who was a likely suspect. What's more, Paul and the others could do nothing about it. Everyone was on short-term contracts anyway and that meant zero rights.

A couple of the blokes had young families to support and were naturally enough doing their nuts. Only a couple of security guards were standing between them and their vocalised desire to kick the store manager's fucking head in. But Paul just left them to it and walked away towards the town centre.

It was a good three mile walk from Supashop to the train station, and the light drizzle wasn't making it any more enjoyable as he made his way along the grass verge that ran alongside the dual carriageway. He could have hung about and got a lift off of somebody, but he had enough problems of his own without having to listen to others moaning.

The only light came from the overhead street lamps, and the only noise from the occasional passing car, but that suited Paul fine. He had a lot of thinking to do and was glad that none of the others had decided to cut their losses and join him on his long walk.

He might not have had a wife and kids to worry about, but things weren't exactly going too well on the domestic front for Paul either. Carol had been back in Hull for two weeks and he hadn't heard so much as a word from her.

Every day had been the same. Home from work around seven in the morning, then a quick bite of breakfast, and then the twenty minute wait for the postman to call before getting some kip. Every morning, he'd waited to hear the sound of his letter box opening and the sound of letters coming through, and every morning he had rushed out to the hallway to be disappointed. All he ever brought back to the kitchen table was bills, more bills and junk mail. "Congratulations Mrs. West - you may have already won £50,000!" Yeah, and Deputy Dawg has been elected President of America.

Paul had given Debbie a bell to find out if anything was wrong, but all she had heard was that Carol got back okay and that was it. He had also told Debbie that he had written to Carol, but what he didn't say was that he'd now written four times. And still no word back.

Loads of thoughts crossed his mind. Maybe she was really busy at work and hadn't had the chance to reply. Or maybe her parents had found one or more of his letters and were giving her a hard time. Or maybe she just wasn't much of a letter writer.

The one thing he refused to believe was that she didn't want to know to him. They might have only been together a short while, but he knew that it had meant something to her, just like it did to him.

The sudden blare of a car's horn caused Paul to almost jump out of his skin. "Up the workers!" shouted Dwayne, leaning out of the passenger door window as he sped by in one of the other lad's cars. Paul just lifted his hand in recognition and watched as the car negotiated the roundabout ahead without the slightest trace of brake lights coming on.

Paul's thoughts quickly returned to Carol. *Why the fuck hasn't the stupid bitch written?*

CHAPTER NINE

FOR the second Saturday in a row, Paul couldn't be bothered with going to the game. Last Saturday, the Gills were away again at Bradford City, but after working a hectic shift Friday night there was no way he could face the long trip to Bradford, even if they were top of the table. Plus a long trip north would have meant putting no money by for Hull.

This Saturday, Gillingham were at home to Bristol City, but what with getting the sack and still no word from Carol, he wasn't in the mood for going anywhere. He hadn't even heard from the others since Tony had left him at the hospital. In fact, since the game at Bolton, the only person he'd seen was little Simon who came to see him after school one day to see how he was doing. So much for all mates together and all that. If that's what the Syndicate had become then he was better off out of it.

When the doorbell rang at just after midday, Paul was still lying in his bed, half sleeping, half thinking about Carol. His Mum answered it, and he recognised Trev's voice from the hallway.

"Paul?" called his Mum through the closed bedroom door. "It's Trevor to see you."

"Yeah, I'll be out in a minute!" he called back before getting out of bed and pulling on a pair of jeans that had been on a heap on the floor since the previous night.

After taking a piss and having a quick wash, Paul found his Mum and Trev having a cup of tea in the kitchen.

"Alright mate," Trev said when he saw his friend appear in the doorway. "Your Mum just told me you got the sack last night! I didn't even know you'd got a job!"

"Yeah, stupid bastards! I was starting to get used to working nights as well."

"Well, you'll just have to see what's down the Jobcentre on Monday," said his Mum as only Mums can.

"Yeah, me and the other three million on the scrap heap!"

"Anyway, you coming to the game today?" Trev asked, changing the subject.

"Yeah, might as well," Paul replied. It was good to see Trev again and going to the game would let him forget about his problems, for ninety minutes anyway. "Give me ten minutes and I'll be ready."

Bristol City had been relegated to the Third Division just the season before and were really too big a club to be stuck in the backwaters of football, and their form said as much. With both them and the Gills still in the promotion hunt, it looked like being a good game and a decent sized crowd was expected.

As Trev and Paul made their way to the Rainham End, they passed by some graffiti that had been on the stadium's wall for two seasons now. In foot high letters, Alan and Colin had painted, DEFEND YOUR MANOR - JOIN THE MSS. All it took was one look at that, and Paul was feeling good again. The adrenaline started pumping and he was looking forward to cracking a few heads if the chance arose.

As they made their way across the terracing to where the other Gillingham skinheads were standing, they noticed a group of about thirty blokes down at the bottom, directly behind the goal. Usually, the only people who stood there were the little kids who spent the game chasing each other around, or the incredibly short-sighted, and it was pretty obvious that these boys didn't fit into either category. All were casuals in their late teens and early twenties, and any of the Rainham End regulars could have told you that they weren't local lads.

"Alright boys," said Alan as Trev and Paul reached their mates. "That's City down there!" he added, pointing to the mob they had already been eyeing up.

"How the fuck did they get in here?" asked Paul, wondering why the police bothered to stand outside the turnstiles if they weren't going to stop away fans getting into the home end.

"No fucking idea," was Alan's reply, "but it saves us going looking for 'em!"

It was still ten minutes to kick-off, and the intruders were keeping quiet, despite the Gillingham chants being bellowed out from the terracing above them. Even taunts of "You must have come on a tractor!" didn't get a response from the cider swilling yokels.

Then, as the players ran out on to the pitch, a cry of "City!" went up and the Bristol mob turned to face the Gillingham faithful. Within seconds, the casuals were crossing the no-man's land of three steps that had opened up between the two sets of supporters, and were running towards their enemy. But almost as quickly, fifty Gillingham fans were in amongst them, stopping the invasion dead in its tracks.

Blows were exchanged, but it quickly became obvious that this was one end that Bristol City wouldn't be taking this season. The City mob had not only made the big mistake of trying to run up terracing when everyone knows it's far easier coming down or along it, but they had also chosen to do it at the precise point where a group of about twenty gypsies had been standing. And when it came to fisticuffs, there was nothing these well dressed upstarts could teach the travellers.

By the time Paul and the others had made their way to the thick of the action, the City casuals were on the retreat, and overweight bobbies were risking heart attacks by running the full length of the pitch from where they had been policing the majority of the away fans.

As the gate in the perimeter fence opened to let the plods into the Rainham End, an uneasy truce was already in place. The City mob was back where it had started, down by the goal, with Gillingham fans calling the Bristol boys forward, and the Bristol boys mouthing back, but not risking another hiding.

Soon the gap that had opened up between the two sets of supporters was filled by a dozen or so police officers who began to escort the Bristol City casuals out on to the pitch and towards the other end of the ground. Chants of "Run away! Run away! Run away!" followed their slow progress as the Rainham End celebrated victory.

Only Swansea and, surprisingly enough, Rotherham had tried to take Gillingham's end so far this season, but neither had enjoyed any success. Millwall had been more interested in rucking in pubs before the game, Derby had come on Boxing Day and without any mob, and the only other team likely to try their luck, Burnley, didn't play at Priestfield until the end of March. In fact, Paul couldn't remember the Rainham End falling since Spurs came and conquered back in '79 during an end of season testimonial match for long time club servant, Graham Knight. That night, Gillingham had been routed by a well organised Spurs mob of around 50 who more than lived up to their trademark "We are evil!" chant.

Not everyone had finished with Bristol City though. One of the gypsies, a real ox of a bloke, ran forward, evaded two policemen and lashed out at one of the casuals. As he continued throwing punches, the police tried to restore order again by pulling him off. One bobby's hat went flying as the gypsy elbowed him in the face as he pulled his arm back to smack the casual yet again.

More police arrived and with the Bristol City fans now through the gate, they decided to try and arrest the gypsy who was still swinging punches at anyone who got in his way.

Just when it looked like the police had him pinned to the fencing and everything back under control, more gypsies decided to rescue their friend and it soon became a stand-up fight between Gillingham fans and the local constabulary. Never one to miss an opportunity like this, Trev decided to join in the fun and within seconds the gypsies were joined by half a dozen skinheads for a bit of plod bashing.

Paul was in there too, kicking out at the thin blue line, half of whom were lashing out with their truncheons while the others acted as snatch squads - two or three officers who grabbed and arrested anyone within reach, whether they were causing trouble or not. Not that they were having any success because as soon as they had someone in their clutches, another five or so Gillingham fans joined in the battle and launched a rescue mission.

The police soon realised they were on a hiding to nothing and, with the game already under way, they decided to retire to the safety of the other side of the fence. The last one through the perimeter gate was helped on his way by Tony's boot up his arse as "Kill the bill!" chants echoed around the ground.

There had been no more trouble during the game, unless you count the Bristol City fans ripping an advertising board off the top of the away end and throwing it on to the grass by the goal-line. With City winning 1-0 at half-time and adding a further two in the second half, Gillingham fans had to be content with cheering Cascarino's only goal in reply and generally taking the piss out of the away end.

Any noise the City fans made in their half of the Town End was lost to the skies. At one point, the Rainham End were going, "Sssshhhh!", as if calling for quiet so that they could hear exactly what the City fans were shouting. But just as silence dawned, an almighty call of "Aaaaargh!" signalled that whatever it was, the Gillingham fans weren't impressed. Indeed for much of the game, the Rainham End had to resort to self-abuse with chants of "We're so shit it's unbelievable!" or baiting the referee who had turned up without his glasses and been unable to see much of the action on the pitch.

When the final whistle brought an end to the scrappy 3-1 home defeat, large numbers of disappointed Gillingham fans quickly made their way to where the away fans would soon be leaving the ground. The loss of three points to promotion rivals, coupled with the trouble in the Rainham End before kick-off, guaranteed aggro after the game.

Paul and the other skinheads made their way along Redfern Avenue under the watchful eye of the police who were determined to keep the two sets of fans apart. Coaches carrying City supporters were brought to the away end so that most of them would be on the motorway west again before they knew it. But it wasn't the coaches that interested the MSS. Few hooligans travelled on official supporters coaches and the chances were that any City fans looking for a rumble would be on their way to the train station.

A shout in the distance alerted both police and skinheads alike that trouble had erupted in a nearby street. Two police vans quickly vacated their parking spaces outside the main entrance to Priestfield and headed off to dispense some law and order, which left the skinheads to make their way along one of the alleyways that criss-crosses the tightly packed terraced houses in the immediate area of the football ground.

Fifty yards ahead in the alley, Paul could see a group of four lads, but they weren't wearing any colours so it was impossible to tell if they were

Gillingham or City fans. The skinheads quickened their pace and were soon right behind their potential targets.

"Excuse me, mate," Trev said, pretending he wanted to overtake.

Without a word, the four blokes stopped and waited for the skinheads to pass. Trevor had passed three before suddenly turning on the fourth and pushing him into the hedges that lined the alleyway. "Fucking City bastard!" he shouted as his fist smashed into the surprised bloke's face.

Paul and the others quickly went to work too, kicking and punching out at the rival fans who were lambs to the slaughter in the tight confines of the alley. A red and white scarf fell out from under one of the boy's jackets, confirming everyone's belief that their silence when letting the skinheads pass had been to avoid giving the game away with West Country accents.

The bloke Paul was booting mercilessly as he crouched on the ground was screaming to be left alone. His pathetic wails made him sound like a little girl and they just encouraged Paul to find the bloke's mouth with his heavy boot in a bid to shut the cunt up.

Alan's victim was lying still on the ground, oblivious to the kicks still reigning in on him. Even the half-brick that Colin had found failed to get a response when it was smashed against his already bloody skull.

With all four City fans beaten to the ground, the MSS boys took their leave by running along the rest of the alleyway, before coming out on to a residential street just a few minutes from the station. Once there, they began walking again as if nothing had happened. From the direction of the station and town centre, they could hear the sound of police sirens, so obviously it had kicked off down there too, but the skinheads had no interest in joining in. With the police in attendance, anyone looking for trouble was a certainty to be lifted.

Instead, they made their way to the Railway Bells for a few pints and to see the rest of the football results. After all, there was certainly no hurry to go home. Alan had found twenty quid in one of the bastard's pockets, not to mention a virtually brand new watch on his wrist, and the next few drinks were on him.

Come Tuesday and it was down to the pub for the regular weekly meeting. The trouble at the Bristol City game hadn't even made the local newspapers, and that night nobody even mentioned the four blokes that had been left for dead in the alleyway. Most of the evening's talk centred around Saturday's trip to Millwall.

Nobody had a bigger reputation in Division Three than the Lions and everyone was looking forward to what for the Gills was the nearest they got to a derby game all season. What's more, Millwall were another club looking for promotion and they had already beaten the Gills 4-1 at Priestfield earlier in the season. In fact, with results like that and the embarrassing 7-1 defeat at York just a month later, it was incredible that the Gills were still talking in terms of promotion.

Ten MSS boys had said they were definites for the trip and with Paul too, that would mean eleven squeezing into Alan's old Transit van for the short journey to the Den. Not the biggest mob to turn up at Millwall, and hardly enough to keep the Junior

Bushwhackers at bay, but the MSS weren't interested in suicide missions anyway. It was just important to make your presence known and then see what you could get away with without putting your name down for a week's worth of hospital food.

After losing to Trev at pool, Paul went over to Debbie who was watching Billy playing the fruit machine.

"Heard anything from Carol?" he asked her.

"No, I haven't, Paul," she replied.

Paul got the impression that she'd rather talk about something else, but God knows nothing else had entered his mind since she had waved goodbye to him from the departing train.

"I was going to give her a ring to see how she's doing," Paul added. "Do you have her number?"

"Yeah, I do," Debbie replied, "But I don't think it's a good idea phoning her." She wanted to tell Paul that Carol was going to get married in a couple of months and what ever they had going while she was down was over with. But of course she didn't. She couldn't just blurt it out there anyway. Not with Billy and the others within earshot.

"She told me what her parents are like, but I ain't bothered. I just need to talk to her." Then he hit Debbie with his master plan. "Maybe you could ring up, and once Carol comes to the phone, pass it to me. That way her parents will just think she's talking to you."

Debbie was looking increasingly flustered and Paul was beginning to wonder what the fuck was going on.

"Debs, get us another pint!" Tony called over from the pool table, and with that she left Paul to watch Billy alone.

Fuck you then, Paul thought. Maybe Carol had said something to Debbie about him, but if she had then the least he deserved was to hear it. Which led him on to plan B. If Debbie wouldn't give him the number, then he would get it from directory enquiries. He had her name and address and would just have to risk calling her himself.

Billy said goodbye to his last coin and then turned to Paul. "How you feeling now, mate, after London?"

"Fine. My ribs are still a bit sore first thing in the morning, but the hospital reckons no permanent damage has been done."

"Good to hear it," Billy replied. "Fancy another pint?"

"Yeah, go on then."

While Billy was at the bar getting the drinks in, he looked over at Paul and thanked God he was all right. If he'd had more bottle, those two blokes wouldn't have laid into him so much, and certainly wouldn't have walked away so easily. Not that he was ever going to tell Paul, or any of the others come to that.

"Oi! put the TV on will you Fred," Tony shouted to the barman. "The football results will be coming on."

Gillingham were playing at Plymouth Argyle and really needed three points to keep up the pressure at the top of the table. Despite everyone's high hopes of the Gills doing the business, the newsreader could only provide a 1-1 draw. Still, better than a slap in the face, and a result at Millwall on Saturday would make all the difference.

Before the night was out, Alan told everyone who was going to Millwall to be outside the Red Lion by ten o'clock sharp or he'd be leaving without them. Nobody wanted to miss this one though, not even Woody who it was rumoured was coming out of retirement to go over the trenches against London's finest.

As he left work on Thursday, Tony was surprised to see Paul waiting for him at the timber yard's gate.

"Alright, mate. What brings you here then?"

"Bored stiff, ain't I?" said Paul. "Wondered if you'd fancy a quick pint or two?"

"Sounds good to me. What about Millwall then?"

As they walked along the road to the nearby pub, the two skinheads talked about nothing else. The previous night Millwall had played Luton Town in the Cup and the match had ended with Millwall fans rioting. It had been top of the bill on yesterday's *News At Ten*, and today the tabloids were full of pictures of Millwall fans on the pitch, ripping up seats and running the police.

As they sat down at a table in the near-empty pub, the riot continued to fuel their conversation. "There's a bloke in the timber yard who was at the game," Tony told Paul. "Millwall daft he is, and he reckons the police were asking for it all night long. First off they kept the Millwall fans in the train station until quarter of an hour before kick-off, and then they crammed them into a part of the ground that would have been full up with half the supporters."

"It's the same everywhere," argued Paul. "They treat away fans like shit, but don't like it when the shit hits the fan."

"Just wait until Saturday. There'll be more police at the game than we've seen all season. The chances of us having a go at anyone is fuck all."

Paul took another gulp from his beer. "Just make sure nobody wears any Gillingham colours. Not even Gillingham boxer shorts. Then once we've parked up the van, we can see what the score is without picking up an escort."

"We'll be wasting our fucking time," Tony replied. "Soon as they clock a skinhead mob we'll attract Old Bill no matter how quiet we are."

Paul could only nod in agreement. Although he wasn't going to say so, maybe that was for the best anyway. After the Luton game, you could guarantee that Millwall would be packed with nutters the following Saturday, all claiming to have been at the game and all looking for an action replay. And there was every chance that the MSS would end up taking a severe hiding. Especially if some of those who said they were going now dropped out because of the media coverage given to Millwall's fans.

"I reckon our best bet is to wait until just before kick-off time, when most people will be inside the ground, including the Old Bill," said Tony, who had obviously been giving it a lot of thought. "And then we can smash up one of their top pubs. That way, we still get to make our mark and will have them going barmy after the game, but don't run the risk of getting lifted by the police."

"Sounds good to me," Paul said, finishing his drink. "Fancy another?"

"Better not, mate," Tony responded. "I'm driving and I said I'd go over and see Debs tonight."

"Has she heard anything from Carol, do you know?"

"Don't think so. You still heard nothing?"

"Nah, fuck all."

"Do you fancy going to a party with me and Debs tomorrow night?" Tony asked, trying to get Paul thinking about other birds. "It's one of her work-mate's 21st birthday bash and should be a laugh."

"Yeah, okay," Paul replied, thinking he had nothing better to do.

"Right, that's settled then. We'll pick you up about eight o'clock okay, my son?"

The one pint he'd had with Tony gave Paul the courage to do what he'd wanted to do all week. He had got Carol's number from the operator after leaving the pub on Tuesday, and now he was standing in a phone box ringing it.

In for a penny, in for a pound, Paul thought as he heard the ringing out sound from the telephone.

"Hello."

"Hello, Carol?" Paul couldn't believe his luck when he heard her voice.

"Yeah."

"It's me, Paul! How's it going?"

There was a slight pause before Carol answered. "I'm fine . . . What are you phoning for?"

"Because I wanted to talk to you! I thought you were going to write . . . Did you get my letters?"

"Yeah, thanks . . . I've just been really busy at work and haven't had time to write back."

"So will you write to me tonight?" Paul asked.

"I'll try. Look, I have to go . . . "

"I really miss you, Carol," Paul said, hoping for some sort of response.

"Yeah, okay then. Bye."

And with that she was gone. Paul didn't know what to think. He certainly wouldn't be needing the handful of pound coins he was hoping to feed into the coin slot. Maybe it just wasn't easy for her to talk to him, especially if her parents were within earshot, but it was beginning to dawn on him that maybe she just didn't want to talk to him full stop.

As he walked home, he kept wishing he had been able to talk to her properly. Doubts about her kept ebbing into his mind, but they were quickly sent packing by other thoughts that told him birds weren't like blokes. To them sex wasn't just about having a good time. It was about love. Or so he was always led to believe anyway. Blokes were the bastards, not girls. And he just couldn't believe that their days together could be simply forgotten, dismissed like a casual one-night fling after three pints too many on a weekend trip to Margate.

Where all this left him, he didn't know. Certainly none the wiser anyway. If she'd told him to get lost, then at least he would have known where he stood. But she didn't. She could have, but didn't. And in Paul's mind, that counted for something.

Carol kissed Ray goodnight and then climbed out of his car. As he pulled away, she returned his wave and then walked along the pathway that led to the back door.

"Is that you Carol?" her Dad called as he heard the back door open and close.

She walked through the kitchen into the lounge to where her parents were watching TV. "Yeah, that's me back."

"Did you have a good time then?" asked her Mum.

"Yeah, it was okay. I'm off to have a bath. Is there any hot water left?"

"Should be plenty, love," her Mum answered.

Laying there in a piping hot bath, Carol thought about what she was going to do. She had known she was definitely pregnant for three days now, but still hadn't told anyone. What was there to tell anyway? With any luck it would all be a mistake and the next time she went to the doctor's he would tell her as much. She could hardly tell Ray she was in the club when she knew full well that the chances were it was Paul's baby she was carrying. And her parents would kill her if they found out.

It was good to hear Paul's voice earlier that evening, even if he did phone when Ray was sitting there, listening to every word she said. She had wanted to forget all about him and concentrate on her future with Ray. That's why she hadn't bothered answering his letters, even if she did feel guilty every time another one arrived. He had now written six times in three weeks. But hearing his voice reminded her what a great time she'd had with him down in Kent.

With the wedding just three months away now, it would have been the easiest thing in the world for her to forget about Paul altogether, but that little pregnancy test kit had changed all that. If things had been different, maybe her and Paul would have got it together, but too many plans had been made to think about him now.

As far as she was concerned, if she wanted to have the baby, then she had to convince Ray that the baby was his. That wouldn't be too difficult either. Since she had got back from staying with Debbie, they had been at it like rabbits, with Ray keen to do the business whether he had come suitably equipped or not. Tonight, on the back seat of his car, he didn't even get the chance to put a Durex on. Carol told him she preferred it without and her frantic whispers for him to come inside her meant he hadn't bothered to waste time putting one on.

Carol was surprised that Tony or Debbie hadn't told Paul about her getting married in the near future anyway. Whatever, she was sure he'd soon get the message that she wasn't interested in him when he still didn't get any reply to his letters.

CHAPTER TEN

FRIDAY morning, and Paul was up at the crack of dawn. He was at the market before most of the stall holders had even started setting out, and he had to wait a good twenty minutes before Alan's van pulled up.

"Alright, my son," Alan said, as he jumped out of the driver's side. "Come to do a decent day's work have we?"

"Yeah, if there's any work going," said Paul, looking to Alan's Dad.

"Course there is," replied the old man. He had a soft spot for Paul, and knew he always got a full day's work out of the boy. "And you can start by getting us all a hot cup of tea. It's bloody freezing today!"

"Tell me about it," replied Paul as he headed off to the catering van. "I've been stood here freezing me balls off waiting for ya!"

Despite the cold, the market was jam packed and the stall had one of its best days since Christmas.. And when it came to three o'clock and pay time, Paul was well pleased to find three brown notes shoved into his hand. Thirty quid for a day's work wasn't bad in anybody's book, especially when the tax man wouldn't be seeing a penny of it.

"Thanks a lot, Mr. Green."

"No worries, son," replied Alan's old man. "Now you two behave yourselves and I'll see you later."

The two skinheads watched as the van pulled away and then headed towards a pub on Rochester High Street. A few beers and a cheese and pickle roll was just what the doctor ordered after a day on the market.

As they walked in to be greeted by the pub's warm air, Paul saw Carl Wallis sitting by himself up at the bar.

"Alright Carl," he said patting his mate on the back. "What you doing here this time of day?"

"Alright Paul," Carl replied, genuinely pleased to see a friendly face in a virtually empty boozer. "Me boss heard about me going to court and sacked me."

"That's a bit steep ain't it," said Alan. "Surely he can't sack ya for something you did outside of work?"

"Yeah, well I told him I was at the dentist when I was at court. Then he read about it in the *Evening Post*, didn't he."

"You soppy bastard," Paul said, shaking his head. "Here, what are you drinking?"

"Pint of lager please, Paul."

The three friends spent another hour or so in the pub before Alan decided it was time he was making a move. "I've got a hot date tonight with this bird who lives in the same street as me," he boasted. "And fuck, can she go!"

"Take it easy then, mate," Paul said. "And save some of that energy for tomorrow!"

"No worries. Catch you two later!"

With Alan gone, Paul asked Carl what he had planned for the evening.

"Nothing much," said Carl who had planned to carry on drowning his sorrows until he ran out of cash.

"How do you fancy coming to a party then with me and Tony. You remember Tony don't you?"

"Yeah, course I do," replied Carl, thinking back to their school days. " Sounds good to me!"

"Right, let's shoot back to my place for something to eat and I can get out of these clothes."

As they approached the front door of Paul's flat, both knew something was wrong. The door wasn't closed properly and the door frame had been smashed where the lock should have held it shut.

Flinging the door open, Paul rushed into the flat, calling out to his Mum. "Mum! Mum! Are you alright?"

He burst into the kitchen and found his Mum sitting at the table, sobbing into a handkerchief.

"What the fuck happened?" he said, looking around at the walls. Everywhere had been sprayed with aerosol paint. FUCK YOU! screamed two big red words above the fridge and other obscenities covered every spare bit of wall surface you could see.

"I came back from the shops this afternoon," his Mum said, "And we'd been broken into. They took the TV and video and some of my jewellery."

Carl came into the kitchen just in time to hear Paul's mother explain what had gone on. He had already been into the living room and it was in a real state. Not content with robbing the place, the bastards had smashed up a display cabinet and everything inside it too. It was mostly worthless stuff, but no amount of money could replace the memories that had been destroyed in what must have been minutes. The spray-can artist had been at work in there too, leaving his mark on the walls, the three piece suite, the carpet, everything.

"Did you call the police Mrs. West?" Carl asked, trying his best to be of some help.

"Yes, they came and took some details, but said it was the seventh burglary they've been called to in as many weeks on the estate and don't expect to get anything back."

"It ain't the TV that matters!" Paul said with real anger in his voice. "Look what the bastards have done to the place!"

"It'll be kids looking for money for drugs," Carl said. "They do the same over my estate."

Paul couldn't stand to see the place looking like this. His Mum had worked hard to keep this council flat looking like a real home since his Dad had died, and some bastard decides to ruin it as part of an afternoon's thieving. He walked past Carl and headed for his bedroom.

"Fucking bastards!" he shouted as he opened his door. His room had been ransacked and his Gillingham poster had been ripped from the wall and left in shreds on the floor. And as a final insult, someone had done a shit on his bed.

Carl soon appeared at his bedroom door and surveyed the mess. "Any idea who has done this, mate?" he asked.

"Take your pick! This estate is crawling with drug-taking scum who would steal from their own mother to get a fix. Come on, let's get out of here!"

Leaving his Mum alone to face up to the aftermath of the break-in wasn't the kindest thing Paul could have done, but he just couldn't stand being in that flat a second longer. Even after downing two pints in record time, he was still feeling as frustrated as he had when he'd seen the mess the bastards had made of his home. Frustrated that there was fuck all he could do to put it right.

Carl came back from the bar with more drinks. "When you find out who done it, mate, give me a shout and we'll get them sorted."

Paul smiled at Carl. He was grateful for his company and appreciated the offer, but he shouldn't have to rely on Carl for back-up. His own skinhead crew should be there for him, but when it came down to it, they never were. Just like in London when he took that kicking in the pub toilets. How nobody noticed what was going on still bothered him, not that he'd said anything. And why the fuck weren't Tony and Debbie helping him with Carol? Some fucking mates they were turning out to be. The more he thought about it, the more he began to think that he was wasting his time in the Syndicate.

"One thing's for sure," Carl continued, "the Old Bill won't do fuck all. Even if they catch them, they'll be out on bail within a day or two doing more houses."

"You ain't wrong there," Paul said as he started on his new pint.

It was a strange conversation to be having. Few people would have expected two yobbos with criminal records to be giving it the big one about law and order, but all the same Paul knew Carl was right. If justice was to be done, he would have to administer it himself.

Anyone who thought different was away with the fairies.

Judging from the middle of the road stodge blaring from the DJ's speakers, this 21st birthday party was definitely a family and friends affair, and the community hall was filled to bursting point with people, young and old.

Paul looked around, but couldn't see Debbie or Tony for the sheer weight of numbers giving it there all on the dancefloor in aid of *The Birdie Song*.

"Here you go, mate," Carl said as he passed Paul a can of beer he'd bought from the makeshift bar in the far corner. "There's some fucking tasty birds over by the bar if you fancy pulling something tonight."

Paul followed Carl's finger and started to laugh. The three tasty birds couldn't have been any older than 12, and all were wearing practically identical party dresses usually associated with kids of five or six.

"If they're old enough to bleed, then they're old enough to breed!" Carl added jokingly.

Just then, Tony made his way through the crowd of middle aged men who were standing by the edge of the dancefloor and laughing at their womenfolk flapping their arms chicken-style. "So you made it then!"

"Alright, mate," Paul replied. "We've just been eyeing up the talent."

Tony looked at the young girls Paul and Carl were nodding in the direction of and smiled. "Yeah, I think one of them's married, but you should be okay with the other two!"

"All set for tomorrow then?" Paul asked his skinhead mate.

"Yeah, Red Lion ten o'clock. Should be a good one!" Tony then turned to Carl and said, "You don't fancy a trip to Millwall do you?"

Carl smiled. "No thanks, Tony. Knowing my recent form, I'll get lifted for dropping litter!"

"Paul was saying about your result at West Malling," Tony said. "Fucking steep weren't it?"

"Try telling that to the old biddy who passed sentence. I think she wanted to get home early so cancelled the cases after mine and gave me a day's worth of fines!"

As the three friends chatted away, Debbie came over with the birthday girl, Jane. Seeing them coming, Tony cut short the joke about the judge and the prostitute, and introduced Jane to his mates.

Jane was a good looking girl and Carl was straight in there with a birthday kiss. And he didn't leave it there either. *Vienna* by Ultravox was the DJ's choice for loving couples everywhere, and before you could say Romeo and Juliet, Carl and Jane were slow dancing their way around the hall.

"Doesn't waste any time does he?" Debbie said to Paul who just smiled in return.

Seeing Carl and Jane whispering into each other's ear had quickly brought home to Paul the fact that he was alone. Worse than that, the girl he wanted was hundreds of miles away and couldn't even be bothered to talk to him on the phone. He wanted to ask Debbie if she'd heard anything, but the bloke had some pride left and didn't want to keep going on about her, especially when he sensed Debbie knew more than she'd been willing to tell him previously.

"Isn't that right mate?"

Paul suddenly became aware that Tony was speaking to him, but he'd not heard a word. "Sorry?"

"I was just telling Debbie that you've got your eye on one of the birds by the bar!"

Tony and Debbie were laughing, and from where Paul was standing it looked like they were laughing at him. Taking the piss because he'd fallen for Carol and they knew she didn't want to know. And now they were saying all he could get was a spotty little kid. "What's so fucking funny?" Paul asked, with a sudden note in anger in his voice.

"Calm down mate," Tony said, seeing that Paul was no longer sharing the joke about the schoolgirls. "I was only pulling your leg!"

Tony went to put his arm on Paul's shoulder in a gesture of friendship, but Paul wasn't having any of it. He stepped back and looked at both Tony and Debbie. "That's it, good old Paul. Always good for a fucking laugh. You make me fucking sick!"

Paul was beginning to sound loud and was attracting looks from some of the other nearby guests. Even Carl caught a glimpse of what was happening and stopped dancing to look over.

"You don't know what you're saying, mate," Tony said. "That's the drink talking."

"Fuck you!" Paul shouted. "Fuck the lot of you bastards! You're all the fucking same! Two-faced bastards!"

By now Jane's father had come over to see what was happening, as had Carl to try and calm his friend down.

"I think it's time you left, young man," Jane's Dad said, pointing towards the door.

"You going to make me then, granddad?" was Paul's reply as he squared up to knock hell out of the man.

Carl and Tony stepped in to stop any fists flying and bundled Paul towards the door.

"Fuck off home and get some sleep," Tony said once they'd got him outside. He was angry that Paul had caused a scene at what should have been a relaxing knees-up for all present.

"So has Debbie heard anything from Carol or ain't I good enough to be told?" Paul asked, still looking for confrontation. "Call yourself friends? You're fucking nothing, you and Debbie. Fucking nothing!"

Tony didn't have to take that sort of lip off of anyone and normally he wouldn't have thought twice about decking anyone for bad mouthing Debbie. But he knew Paul had had far too much to drink, and he also knew deep down that they had let Paul down. "I'll forget you said that. Now piss off home and make sure you're outside the Red Lion at ten o'clock sharp or we're leaving without you!"

"I ain't fucking going nowhere with you," Paul shouted as he began to walk away from the hall. "You're fucking nothing! Fucking nothing! The Syndicate is full of fucking pussies!"

Tony just shook his head as he saw Paul walk away into the night.

"He ain't had the best of days," Carl said as he waited with Tony to make sure Paul was pissing off home and wasn't going to come back in for more aggro. "His flat got turned over this afternoon and all he talked about in the pub was that bird Carol."

"Yeah, well he might as well forget her," Tony said as they both walked back into the hall where Debbie and Jane were waiting for them. "That slapper ain't going to do him no good. He don't know it, but she's getting married to a bloke from up her way in a few months so he doesn't have a look in."

Carl looked at Tony. "How comes you ain't told him then?"

Tony just looked at the ground. "It's a long story mate, but to be honest I don't think he'd thank me now even if I did tell him."

"Well, look who it ain't?"

Paul was stopped in his tracks by three blokes standing in his way. He recognised them instantly as some of the boneheads from the scooter dance of a few weeks previously.

"Where's your fucking mates now then?" said the bonehead with the celtic cross sewn on to the front of his black pilot jacket.

Paul said nothing. He was feeling lousy from all the drinking and couldn't be bothered answering.

The bonehead shoved Paul backwards. Then shoved him again. "Come on then, let's have it!"

Paul didn't even resist the shoves. He certainly was in no condition to take on three of them and was resigned to taking a hammering.

"Ain't so fucking hard now are ya!" the bonehead shouted into Paul's face. "You're a fucking tosser that's all!"

Another one of the boneheads came up to Paul. "It ain't our style, three on to one, but if you and your mates want another go, just tell them to name the place and we'll fucking do you so badly you'll wish you hadn't been born!"

Paul stood there, wondering if this was some sort of joke. If him and two others of the Syndicate had caught up with some bastard who had knocked shit out of them a few weeks earlier, they would have kicked him up and down the road like a football. And yet here were three members of the Hitler Youth giving him a mouthful and a lecture on gang law.

As they left Paul to go on his way, one of them did give him a boot in the thigh to speed him up, but that was it. Maybe the world didn't have it in for him after all.

Paul had walked all the way home, and the cold night air coupled with a five mile trek and the run-in with the Nazi skinheads, had done a lot to sober him up by the time he reached his flat. The damage caused by the forced entry could still be seen and he hardly had to turn his key before the door swung open.

It was now three o'clock in the morning, and when he entered his room he could see that his Mum had done her best to tidy things up. A clean bedspread covered his bed and she had even managed to salvage most of his Gillingham poster and stick it back up with his silk scarf. On the floor she had piled up the records that hadn't been smashed, but by the looks of them none could be described as being in the mint condition Paul had always tried to keep them in.

He sat down on his bed and held his head in his hands. As he did so, he realised that the bastards in the flat above were playing their music at full volume again. Only this time, Paul recognised the thudding tune. Sitting up, he looked over at the pile of vinyl his Mum had gathered together and realised that what he was hearing was one of his own records.

Getting to his feet, Paul grabbed his baseball bat and flew out of the flat and up the stairs to the sixth floor. He could hear the music clearly now and recognised Prince Buster's *Rough Rider* immediately. Anger raged through his body as he put one and one together and realised that it was the junkies in the flat above him who had turned over his poor mother's flat. He was going to kill them for this. Fucking kill them. He kicked at the door and saw it shudder in its frame. Then, taking a step backwards, he kicked out again, and the door opened wide.

The flat was full of the sound of the Prince. You would have to be deaf or dead not to hear it at that volume. The rooms were identical in layout to Paul's, and he quickly made his way to the lounge where he could tell the music was coming from.

The room was a fucking tip. Beer cans, crisp packets, dirty ashtrays, fish and chip papers everywhere. The inside of a dustbin lorry looked cleaner. The walls were covered in graffiti and the stench suggested that no windows had been opened for months. It was enough to make Paul feel sick, it really was.

Out for the count in the chair by the record player was one of the filthy hairy bastards who had noised Paul up in the downstairs lobby the previous week. Drink, drugs, whatever it was, this particular piece of human shit was oblivious to the world, let alone Paul standing over him. The record player was automatically playing the same album, over and over, just as it no doubt had done every other night Paul had been kept awake by these bastards.

The modern day hippy didn't even flinch when Paul's bat smashed into his face, once, twice, three times. That's all it took for it to be beaten to a pulp. Paul then, ripped the needle off his record, and smashed the hi-fi to pieces. Sparks flew as his trusty bat made sure it would never make another noise again.

Paul caught his breath and looked at the wanker he had just wasted. Then for good measure, Paul took out his dick and pissed all over the battered hippy's unconscious carcass.

What would have been his bedroom was empty, but as he pushed open the door to the main bedroom door and switched on the light, he could see a naked girl frantically trying to wake her boyfriend from his drug-induced coma. On seeing Paul standing there, she began to scream hysterically, grabbing at the blankets to cover her tits. The stupid bitch didn't have a pair worth hiding. She looked no older than the schoolgirls at the party and here she was shacked up with a fucking druggy.

"Get out the fucking bed!" Paul screamed at her, but she stayed there, frozen with panic, pleading to be left alone.

Paul grabbed her by the hair and pulled her out of the bed, leaving her on the floor screaming at Paul to leave them alone. The unshaven face of her boyfriend began to show signs of life as his heavily tattooed body sat up in the bed. Paul didn't give him the chance to find out what was going on though. Before he had even opened his eyes, Paul swung his bat into the druggy's face with enough force that you could hear the cheek bone splinter on impact.

After that blow, the bastard was going nowhere, and with the little girl still screaming for him to leave them alone, Paul pulled away the blankets and smashed the bat into the pathetic bloke's private parts. The force with which he connected guaranteed it would be a very long time before he'd be shafting anyone again.

The girl was now sobbing uncontrollably, and to get her attention Paul had to grab her face in his hand and hold it an inch away from his own face. "If the pigs ever come looking for me for this, I'm going to come after you, okay? So keep your fucking mouth shut! You didn't see anything okay?"

The girl just looked at Paul, her eyes full of fear.

"I said, okay?"

The added anger in Paul's contorted face saw the girl nodding in agreement.

He pushed her away, leaving her lying on the filthy carpet, trying to preserve any dignity she still had by pulling her discarded jeans over her body.

"You can tell lover boy there that if he ever messes with me again, I'll fucking kill him!"

Paul left the bedroom and returned to the squalid atmosphere of the lounge. The hippy he'd battered earlier was still motionless in the seat, his face covered in a mixture of blood and piss, making it unlikely that even his own mother would have recognised him. If in fact cunts like him ever had a mother.

Paul looked around, but couldn't see his TV or video. Both had no doubt already been sold for a few quid each to pay for the scum's latest hit. He then picked up four albums that he recognised as his, and made his way out of the flat.

CHAPTER ELEVEN

PAUL woke up suddenly. Daylight was breaking through a crack in the curtains and a quick look at his watch told him it was ten past eight. He could here the distant sounds of his Mum in the kitchen and then remembered the state the flat was in following the burglary.

He knew he should get up and help his Mum finish cleaning the place up, but he just couldn't face it. He'd had enough of living in the Medway towns and wanted to get out. No job, no money, and still there was always some bastard waiting to shit on you. Well, he'd had enough and was only too willing to leave behind what little he had to start afresh somewhere else.

The argument with Tony flashed into his mind. He knew Tony was one of the best mates he could ever hope to have, and now regretted what he'd said to him. He wondered what he would say if he turned up at the Red Lion. Probably nothing. It wasn't the first barney they'd had and it wouldn't be the last either.

But Paul had no intentions of going to Millwall today. Not because he didn't want to face Tony, but because he wanted away. He had enough money to get himself up to Hull, and that's what he was going to do. Carol could hardly not talk to him if he turned up on her doorstep, and it might bring home to her just how much he really did care for her.

It was half past nine by the time Paul had got washed, dressed and finished his cup of coffee. His

Mum had offered to cook him a fry up, but after yesterday's session, food was not a pleasant thought, especially if it was served swimming in grease.

As he strolled to the telephone box a short walk from the flats, he turned around and looked up at where he lived and the net curtains that filled his windows. At least he'd sorted out the scum from the flat above. They wouldn't be in any hurry to turn his flat over again, that was for sure.

The sun was shining, and as he walked along in his boots, jeans, braces and white and blue Fred Perry, he was beginning to feel good about what he had decided. He would ring Carol and tell her he was on his way up to Hull that day. And if she didn't want to see him again fair enough, but she would have to tell him to his face. That way he wouldn't go all the way up there to find her family had fucked off for the weekend or something, leaving him on the doorstep looking like a prize lemon when nobody answered. It would also give Carol a chance to tell her parents about him.

An old lady was just leaving the phone box as Paul approached, and he held the door open for her while she came out.

"At least it's working today, son," she said.

"Miracles do happen then!" Paul replied, knowing it was something of a national lottery to find a telephone box that hadn't been vandalised or wasn't 999 calls only.

Taking the piece of paper with Carol's number on it out of his pocket, he picked up the receiver and began to dial. Butterflies filled his stomach and for a moment he thought about just slamming the phone down, but he knew that if he wanted something in this life he had to make it happen. The worst that could happen was that her Mum could answer the phone. And that's exactly what happened.

"Hello," the women's voice said.

"Hello," Paul said hesitantly. "Can I speak to Carol please?"

To his surprise, the woman didn't sound like the ogre she had been made out to be at all. "No, I'm sorry, she's gone out shopping. Can I take a message for her?"

"Yeah, can you tell her Paul from Gillingham rang and that I'll give her a ring later."

"Right, okay," Carol's Mum replied. "She's gone into town this morning and then is going to see Ray, so probably won't be back until tea time, okay?"

Ray? Who the fuck was Ray? He had to ask. He just had to. "Who's Ray?"

"Her fiancé . . . "

The word hit Paul like a ton of bricks, but before he could react or say something, the pips sounded to tell him his money was running out. He fumbled about in his pocket and pulled out a fifty pence piece which the slot gratefully accepted - and then the line went dead.

Paul banged the telephone to try and get his money back, but he had lost it. He searched his pockets for another coin, but found nothing. He banged the coin box in frustration, but still it refused to give him back his money.

That fucking bitch! Paul thought, the anger welling up inside of him threatening to smash the telephone box to pieces in his bid to get his lost coin back. He deserved to know what the fuck was going on with Carol. His mind was full of so many questions, and just as he was beginning to get some answers, British Telecom steals his money!

As he continued to bang his fist against the cold metal, he saw a soap dodger walking past. He recognised him as one of the scruffs who lived in the flat he'd turned over last night, only he hadn't been there during Paul's little visit.

Paul opened the door and ran at the grubby looking youth. He grabbed him by the collar of his German army parka and began shaking him. "Give me your fucking money you bastard! I want your fucking money!"

The youth quickly delved into his left coat pocket and pulled out a five pound note and held it out for Paul. "That's all I've got - take it!"

But a five pound note was of fuck all use to Paul. He shoved the guy to the ground and sat on his chest, his eyes wide open with rage. "I want fucking coins you bastard! Give me all your fucking money!" To make sure he got the message, Paul started to bang the poor cunt's head off the ground.

It obviously did the trick because within seconds, the youth was emptying his pockets out on to the floor. A ten pence piece began to roll away towards the grass, and Paul got up and scrambled after it as if it was gold itself.

Turning from the kid on the deck, Paul ran back to the phone box like a man possessed and quickly dialled a number. His mind was racing, his heart beating faster than ever.

"Come on! Come on!" Paul screamed as he waited for an answer.

"Hello, Medway Taxis. Can I help you?"

"Yeah, I want a taxi from the Oak Point flats to the Red Lion in Gillingham . . . "

"Five minutes?" asked the voice.

"Yeah, great. The name's West - I'll be waiting by the entrance."

The kid was still refilling his pockets as he nervously watched Paul come out of the telephone box. He got to his feet as Paul approached and began to walk backwards, away from the skinhead. "I don't want any more trouble, mate."

"So don't fucking mess with the MSS!" Paul shouted as he headed for where he'd told the taxi to pick him up. When he got back from Millwall, he'd have to unpack his bags because he wasn't going anywhere. *What a fucking prick I've been*, Paul said to himself, knowing that he'd have to apologise to Tony for mouthing off at the party. *Wait until he hears that the fucking bitch is getting married . . .*

THE END

The Return Of Joe Hawkins

Back in the 1970s, Richard Allen was the undisputed king of youth cult fiction. In total, he wrote 18 novels that documented the changes faces of British youth, from the million selling *Skinhead* right through to *Glam* and *Punk Rock* and ending with *Mod Rule*. Sadly Richard Allen, whose real name was James Moffatt, died in 1993, but he lives on through his books which are currently being republished by S.T. Publishing in volumes of three.

THE COMPLETE RICHARD ALLEN VOLUME ONE
Skinhead Suedehead Skinhead Escapes

Three great novels in one book. SKINHEAD portrays with horrifying violence all the terror and brutality that has become the trademark of these teenage malcontents. SUEDEHEAD sees Joe Hawkins grow his hair and swap his boots and braces for a velvet-collared Crombie. And in SKINHEAD ESCAPES, Joe is on the run from prison and looking for aggro!

THE COMPLETE RICHARD ALLEN VOLUME TWO
Skinhead Girls Sorts Knuckle Girls

Three more great novels in one book. SKINHEAD GIRLS gives a girl's eye-view of living for kicks. Joan Marshall was a skinhead at fifteen with all the savagery and excitement that went with it. SORTS are the Smoothies' girls. On the run from home, her skinhead lover and her memories, Terry Hurdy finds herself in a world of sex, drugs - and murder! And finally, meet Glasgow's Ina Murray in KNUCKLE GIRLS. She fights for her rights with a bicycle chain surrounded by a circle of cheering supporters!

THE COMPLETE RICHARD ALLEN
VOLUME THREE
Trouble For Skinhead Skinhead Farewell
Top-Gear Skin

Another three great novels in one book. In TROUBLE FOR SKINHEAD, Joe Hawkins finds himself banged up in Dartmoor and face to face with arch-rival, Charlie McVey. In SKINHEAD FAREWELL, Joe blazes his way across Australia in a bid to nail his old enemy, Charlie McVey, once and for all. And in TOP-GEAR SKIN, meet Roy Baird, the leader of a skinhead gang who need more excitement than pulling birds and putting the boot in has to offer. For him, it's stockcar racing and he'll do anything to win! This volume also include a tribute and interview with Richard Allen.

THE COMPLETE RICHARD ALLEN VOLUME FOUR
Boot Boys Smoothies Terrace Terrors

First there were skinheads. Then came suedeheads. Now there are BOOT BOYS, ready to do battle on the terraces every Saturday afternoon. SMOOTHIES are the new villains of the peace, born out of the skinhead-suedehead cult. The aggro is always present - until they go too far! Then comes TERRACE TERRORS. Who better to tame the football hooligans than Steve Penn and his crew of skins, suedes and boot boys from another era.

By the time you read this book, Volumes Five and Six may also be available. For a complete list of current titles, please write to S.T. Publishing, P.O. Box 12, Dunoon, Argyll. PA23 7BQ. Scotland.

It's 1977. The safety pin is a fashion accessory. The swastika something far more dangerous.

ENGLAND BELONGS TO ME

Derek Peterson is just another bored teenager, hanging around street corners in the Queen's Jubilee year. While everyone else seems to be ripping their trousers and screaming anarchy, Derek tries to stay true to his skinhead roots. But it's easier said than done when he meets a punk bird called Suzi. Together they take a brutal rollercoaster ride through the underground world of punk rock and extremist politics, where the only law is that of the urban jungle. The only justice, an eye for an eye, a tooth for a tooth.

Steve Goodman's debut novel is the literary equivalent of a smack in the face. Not the sort of book you want to buy your old granny.

The above books are available from select outlets or direct from the publisher. For a mail order catalogue please write to S.T. Publishing, P.O. Box 12, Dunoon, Argyll. PA23 7BQ. Scotland.

NON-FICTION FROM S.T. PUBLISHING

Spirit Of '69 - A Skinhead Bible by George Marshall
168 page book packed with photos and cuttings. This book gives the first detailed account of the skinhead cult from the late Sixties to the present day, with chapters on skinhead reggae, 2 Tone, Oi!, today's scene, fashion and lots more. Welcome to the land of the bovver brigade!

Skins by Gavin Watson
The ultimate skinhead photo book with 150 black and white professionally taken photographs of skinheads from the late Seventies and early Eighties. Includes some classic shots.

Total Madness by George Marshall
120 page book with colour and black and white photos charting the rise and fall of Camden Town's favourite sons, Madness. It takes you from the days when the band were still known as The Invaders, right through to the decision to reform in 1992. Includes full discography.

Bad Manners by George Marshall
52 page booklet with black and white photos telling the story of Bad Manners, the band who hit the charts with classics like *Lorraine*, *Lip Up Fatty*, *Special Brew* and lots more. A must for Manners fans. Limited edition of 1,000 printed.

Watching The Rich Kids by Arthur Kay
104 page book with photos destined to become a street classic. Arthur Kay takes you on a tour of the backstreets of rock n' roll which he knows only too well. Includes material on cult ska favourites, The Originals, and the Oi!some Last Resort.

We also have some great books in the pipeline, some of which may already be available by the time you read this. For example, pencilled in for 1994 are books on The Specials, skinhead reggae, The Business, The Oppressed and Oi!. For a copy of our mail order catalogue please write to S.T. Publishing, P.O. Box 12, Dunoon, Argyll. PA23 7BQ. Scotland.

A Message To All Readers

First of all, thank you for buying this book and we hope you found it entertaining. Your comments on this book are always appreciated and can be sent to the address below.

The sole aim of S.T. Publishing is to document street life, both in fiction and non-fiction. If you fancy yourself as a budding Richard Allen or have always wanted to write a book about a band, youth cult, football violence or whatever, then please get in touch. If you have an idea for a book, but don't want to write it yourself, then let us know too.

Sociology students, hack journalists and Swindon Town supporters need not apply.

Our address is S.T. Publishing, P.O. Box 12, Dunoon, Argyll. PA23 7BQ. Scotland.